Of Elegant Time

Of Elegant Time

22 stories

Paula Friedman

2022

PNF Books

USA

PNF Books
1010 SE Ninth Street Gresham, OR 97080 USA

Cover art and book design by
Impress Design | www.i-d.design

This is a collection of works of fiction. With the exception of historical events and personages, all incidents, names, and characters are fictional, despite any resemblance any reader may see to some actual events or persons.

Print Edition 2022, printed and bound in USA
Hardcover ISBN-13: 978-1-7376796-0-8
POD ISBN-13: 978-1-7376796-1-5
Epub ISBN-13: 978-1-7376796-3-9

Dedicated to my parents, Melvin Hillard Friedman and
Beatrice Patricia Friedman

Acknowledgments

"Yosemite" was first published, as "The Little One," in *Earth's Daughters*, no. 57: 2001: An Earth Odyssey

"For Lucie" appeared in *New Flash Fiction Review*, 2018

"The Workings of the Flashlight in the Darkness" was a finalist for the 2017 New Millennium Writing Fiction Award

"The Prayer" was first published, in different form, in *The Open Cell*, no. 3, 1969

"The Kickball Queen of Benjamin Smirch" first appeared in the *Jewish Women's Literary Annual* 4, 1998

"Berkington" was a finalist for the 2019 New Millennium Writing Fiction Award. An earlier version was published in *The Open Cell*, no. 2, 1969

A very different version of "The Man in the Creek" forms the opening segment of my novel *The Rescuer's Path* (2018 [1st ed 2012], PVP)

"Chasing Leads" was first published as part II, chapter 2, of my novel *The Change Chronicles* (2020, PNF Books [2018, Lillicat Publishers])

"A Tale of the Sixties" appeared, as "You asked 'What was happening then?'" in *Viet Nam Generation* 6, 1994, receiving a Pushcart Prize nomination. A later version, "God's Eyes," was a 1996 finalist in the New Millennium Writing Awards

"Sentience" won the 2014 Valentine's Day Award of *Morgen Bailey's Blog*, and was a finalist for the 2016 New Millennium Writing Short-Short Fiction Award

"Reunion" was first published in *Touched by Adoption*, ed. Nancy Robinson (1998, Green River Press), and has also been published in Adoption Constellation (2014, Adoption Mosaic)

"Wait" first appeared, as "Roses, roses," in *Work: A Literary Journey*, 1995-1996

"Jenny's Garden" won the Science Fiction Microstories Contest, June 2017

"Urrrr . . ." was published in *Quantum Tao*, 1997

TABLE OF CONTENTS

On the Trail

Yosemite

With probably only days until my own turn, feeling already the symptoms, I'd say those were the people but what I mourn most was—tritely enough—Yosemite, where, as a young man, I guided, and I remember most two times it pierced my soul.

One evening in the Valley, slipping from the cedars something glided, large and darkling like a creature of science fiction but finally I recognized it was a bird, the head white and feathered—and the great bald eagle flew across the sky where, far above, hung the high country, silences of boulders, limned glacier tarns.

Words don't mourn.

Years later, somewhat stiffly I was biking one spring morning, again in the Valley, for no particular reason below the cliffs, and decided to park and climb the trail to Yosemite Falls. These two women were approaching—grey-haired, my own age (getting up there yet not even sixty, then). One, who wore a fading blue tee-shirt over rather baggy jeans, asked "What, you decided to ride down?" I laughed and said "It's harder going up but faster coming back," and they laughed too and went on. After locking the bike to one of those racks, I started out—there were about two hundred switchbacks—and not far along, still among thick brush and darker rock, I caught up. The little one, the one who'd spoken before, apparently was short-winded and often had to rest. I decided to keep them company, at least part way, have some company myself; we got to talking. I explained how it'd been, how I'd been avoiding people, how I needed time off on my own.

"You working too hard there, huh?" the little one joked. I'd said I was from Seattle. "My office follows me too."

"No, no, it's . . . emotionally difficult." We kept puffing along, the whole time climbing back and forth up the stone-bordered trail.

"What do you work in?"

"Public health." Then I decided to say it. "AIDS. I work with people with AIDS."

She said, "That's hard." She had a relative, it turned out, in the field.

I told her I'd lost so many—that was how it seemed then (in those years before the first pandemic)—"but now my closest friend is dying, it's been going on and on, I needed to get away from it for a few days."

The other woman gave the little one a glance, but she pretended not to notice.

Still, she was careful of her friend (whose name was Martie), and at every opportunity made sure that this Martie, a freckled woman who turned out to really *be* a quiet archivist, shared in the conversation. Where the path straightened and ran along a ledge, we all put on sunblock and those wide-brimmed hats and took one another's snapshots.

"Uncool." The tiny woman's comment took me aback. Then I peered closer at the longish hair and no make-up—sure, this one could have been an ex-hippie.

She caught my look, and pretty soon I was telling them (we were climbing again) what it was like, handling wounded in Nam, catching on to the waste of life there, and how much the protests back home had meant to certain of us.

"Thank you," I said, thirty-odd years later.

She grinned back at me, and in the same instant was laughing. She practically doubled over—leaning on Martie, who supported her, concerned—caught up in a sort of quiet hysterics. I must have looked stupidly puzzled.

"Three old fogeys on the trail in Yosemite," gasped the little one. "Having '60s nostalgia."

Not far after this, there was a stretch where the trail got very slippery and rough, and I found myself giving them each a hand. Then they stopped and rested "just for a minute." I surprised myself by halting, too, instead of going on.

The little one said, "That's good. I'm glad we've a companion of the trail." That's certainly one way I'd never seen myself, as a companion of the trail. As Dave would surely have been willing to attest. Even though I was there, finally, by his side.

Through Their Growing

For Lucie

Well yeah, it's not what you usually find between the snap peas and the new organic bean sprouts. I wasn't buying veggies by intent, besides; I'd planned old-fashioned for tonight: small steaks (t-bone!), mashed potatoes, retro as a dog outside a picket fence signed "Lassie, come on home."

Right. So there it was, all the while I was staring down the aisle and seeing Lucie, Lucie my beloved Lucie lass, so tiny, blond as chicken, soft as everything I wanted in a woman but, as happens when you come on your ideal, I wasn't, as she told me, hers. Okay, and so I blinked and saw fluorescents—saw the dimmed (to save Vanishing Resources!) pale lights; I saw the frozen chickens far away, and turkeys, baby quail, ducks, red-blue canned goods stacked beyond on pallid shelves. *Well, get over the lightbulbs,* said Lucie, and *Jeesh!* and *Things change.*

Again I blinked, tears to my lashes, thinking Lucie, Lucie, I'd have loved you, loved our baby (we'd have had a baby), I could have been good to you. Re-blinked. Looked down.

It was there.

A month old? Two? Three weeks? At any rate, alone. Unblanketed—or rather, wrapped up in a yellow fleecy thing. And waving, as if cilia, its little and not chubby (actually I hate them chubby) arms.

"Goo-goo." Who said "goo-goo"? Not I. No not I, said the father to the sky. Up to the sky, his camera like an eye, eye high in the sky—or on a scaffold, maybe, there behind those tiles along the ceiling panels, watching. Yes, was anybody watching? "Goo," I answered. Decided.

My neckerchief was like a cowboy's, sort of—red white green. I twisted it away, kept back my head, and held my shoulders down. No hunching, nothing one bit strange— no way I'd give away the game. I bagged my bean sprouts, put two heritage tomatoes in a green organic produce sack, picked up the child wrapped in its fleecy, squeezed it tight, and, looking neither left nor right, took three steps to the main aisle, headed toward the check-out stand.

O Lucie, Lucie, what I've got (I glanced about, but super-fast, and just enough to see no mama type around). O Lucie lovely, lovely what I've found us. Love, O squeeze again, a miracle.

Across The Border

"Be quiet, shut up—you want they hear us?"
Mama's angry I cried. She is gone with a Big Man.

All the Mamas are gone. I don't like it here.
The kids say "Shut up, crybaby!" The Big Men shout.
I'm cold.
Mama.
She isn't here, she's somewhere else. The wire makes
walls. There's no potty here. I can't get out. *Where's Mama?*
No, I won't put nappie on. The big kids laugh, say
"Baby, baby."
Mama! Wanna blankey
Juana says, "Don't cry, makes Big Men worse." Juana's
necklace is yellow-green. She is my friend.

She is six-and-a-half. A big girl. She holds me at night on our mat, so we're not afraid. "Here," she says, "use the big people's potty." She shows me how. We are not afraid. We are not cold, we share her blankey. ("'Share,'" she teaches me. "We learn Englush").

Juana is gone with a Big Man. Just like Mama. He came with his key, he took Juana out. She didn't cry, she didn't turn around.

I'm cold. Want Juana.

Mama. Mama was angry 'cause I cried. On the road, in the hot place. And three Big Men came. No, four. I know, 'cause nowdays I can count.

Tomorrow, they say, I am old enough. A Big Man's gonna take me.

"You get to stay with a *Family*," Anna says. Anna is a Big Lady. A Big Man stands behind her, and he watches. He watches four of us, me, Consuela, and Marya, and Orna. Orna says, "I ain't going, I ain't going." The Big Man watches Anna and another Big Lady line us into the bus.

*

One sunset in the summer garden, we were making flower wreaths, Mama picking the lilacs hanging like they never, here. She was brushing my hair and put an extra barrette, saying "Now we'll be journeying, Tonia." If that really was Mama. Plaiting my hair, tying a bow for our new wreath.

Or was that Mrs. Garner? I can't remember. Way back then, I was too little, Mrs. Garner says. "But don't you worry, sweetheart. I'm your Mama now." She likes us all, unless Orna acts up, but it's me she puts on her lap. I'm her *favorite* little girl.

And today was our Anniversary Party. "Y'all been with me a whole year," she says. She smiles and we blow out candles on the cake. It's pretty and pink, and Mrs. Garner's sweet and brown. "Look here," she says, "my eyes are blue." She hugs me tight and smiles and smiles. I love Mrs. Garner.

*

"Tomorrow you get to ride the airplane back home," Mama Garner says. She stands me right next to her knees, takes her winter sewing on her lap. "I'm gonna miss you, sweetheart." I love when Mama Garner calls me sweetheart, I love the times she sings. Only, now what's she mean?

"*This* be our home, Mama Garner."

"Back home, sweetheart. You're going *back home*. With your real Mama."

Who left—I do remember—with a Big Man. 'Cause the Big Men found us, 'cause I cried. That Mama can't even talk Englush.

"*No*, Mama Garner. Please." *I love you.* "I'll be good, I promise."

I'll never, ever cry again.

The Workings of the Flashlight in the Darkness

Through the window, I swirl the flashlight beam across the darkness of our yard. No one. I let the curtain fall.

For two months—since the rainy afternoon we came back after shopping to discover mud strewn through the little house, possessions flung about, the window broken by your bed—I have known this dark, unsettling fear. Only days after the burglar came, our latest housemate fled; we are alone, mother and three-year-old son. If someone breaks in, there'll be no chance to use the phone, my screams won't stir the neighbors; even were there time, how could I hide you safely, Jesse, and what if you cry?

This is the constant danger into which I've borne you—here, in this rented slum house that you babble of so happily, "This one *our* home," where now, in ignorance of all such matters, you are hopping, dancing.

You're delighted by my novel movements with the flashlight—by the very workings of the flashlight. Curious, you laugh aloud, excited, as you climb the rocking-chair, prepare yourself to jump. "Agin, agin! Watch Jesse, Mama, watch me, I do *this* now!"—reach out your arms. Your hair glows, haloed by the light. I lift my hands, pulled by your happiness.

And see, behind you in the dark, the waiting rectangle—curtained, close—of our front window. At any moment, at *this* moment, some intruder may rush in, even upon *you* in your responsive content, your trust in life.

I sit back heavily. Stilled, far across the room from you, in our stuffed chair.

Fear stifles my response. The contrast of your vulnerable love with what can happen in this world, with what I've done to you, and with each outside evil, weights my eyes and arms, again constrains my soul. Knowing I must prevent another evening like last night, carefully I withdraw.

For two hours now, I've left you to your own devices. I've snapped "Now let me clean the house" each time you've run up for a hug, have answered "Read it to yourself" when you've brought me a book. Fear has dampened my stirs of admiration as, ranging your stuffed bears and seals around your chair, you've "read" to them from memory in a crooning teacher's voice, playing the adult I need to be.

But there is no work left, and exhaustion has absorbed much of the fear. I lift you up; I hold you, force a smile, and (with an old surprise) see happiness beam from your eyes. I watch as you suck slowly on your bottle; I rock you gently—and, in this long moment, unexpectedly, I see, in those serious, interested eyes of a young toddler, the huge dark, trusting orbs of the newborn you once were. I feel, within our bodies' present warmth, the unity we knew, those first weeks—before the two months we were parted when I thought I must give you, too, for adoption.

Only for this moment, I can open to the tenderness, the awe, our love of those first weeks. It is the overwhelming, utter love that certain music—less the joyful Brandenburgs than the Pachelbel Canon in D, or the first several notes of one Corelli mass—may momentarily evoke. It is the love that—busily praying to protect you, eyes fixed on each crushing thing about to fall or fallen on us—my desperation's ever veiled, thus enclosing us within a shadow world where any gentle hug may twist into a squeeze, each tender touch turn to a slap, and even the softest gaze, as if traversing circus mirrors or a hundred garish panes of terror and the thousand glittering cobweb strands of desperation, may metamorphize to a stare that fixes on you as upon some stranger child who's somehow happened in, some little child I barely know or knew too long ago, some creature who, though clinging close to me, must stay forever separate.

That is, here is a love so deep that fear (as love brings

fear) has nearly grown complete. For I cannot protect you, Jesse. And some form of fear has parted us each day since you were born. Only the rare moments' cherishing come close to make up for those times—last night and every other time—I've turned on you.

And yet, isn't it true such times come less since we moved to this house? Here, no one threatens or condemns if you act like a child or cry. Now, as when you grew within my womb, I may hold a strong protective shield above you and, when we are challenged—when a supermarket clerk demands "You make that child behave," or we are ordered from a restaurant or other "adult" space—I find strength to strike back with only modulated anger, strictly outward strife, and I no longer fall into those acts—tearful, near-parodic—that, spinning upon you, formed for so long my only, desperate, way to say "Is *this* what you people want? See what you do to love! Look what you force us to!" and cry, as if a beaten animal, belly up where simpler, less impassioned speech will not be heard, for mercy on us.

But—I am sorry—such seeming "modulation," "change," "improvement" must mislead. For it is contingent. In the danger of our nights, we remain vulnerable; I still—in a cycle of swift anger and apology familiar to you as our games out at the park or the geography along our daily routes—turn upon you; last night *happened*.

In fact, if there has been any change—if, as myths of motherhood would hold, my new articulateness indicates a growth, paced to your own, of speech, or if, as one view claims, my misdirected thrashings were but ordinary steps along the road toward insight, revolution, song—this change comes glacially slow. If I have learned a vivid truth or two about my fears for you, still such growth itself, like those very fears (and everything about this Mommy you have known) are rooted, deeply, thickly, in the dark soil of a single night almost four years ago.

That night, while you lay curled up in my womb that, after many hours, still kept cramping from the amniocentesis, I came to a point of choice: I might "trust, take what comes," or I might cry for help. But to cry out meant to acknowledge danger to you, meant to know a fear and feel a rage (at those, myself included, who had led us to this risk) and helplessness I'd never felt before. It meant to recognize how much the smallest danger to you mattered, how much *you* mattered.

Leaning on my elbows, staring at the pillow and the waxed boards of the floor, with the gentlest of motions I began to turn, and, inside, you too turned; the single choice was made.

Or rather, I had "jumped"—a sort of slippage had occurred—from some established balance point; there was a letting go of everything but you. And—*one* with you in this new, vulnerable universe where, since, we live—I understood, beside the heightened danger and deepened fear, the blessing of your life, of life.

However, it was at this point—as if no more were occurring than the leap from resignation to awareness that

I must fight for you—I first called out (and could not cease to call) for help. Yet, in knowing there was little anyone could do, I saw already what I've known, so often, since—what we must each, at moments, know—the life-and-death is not in human hands.

I mean that in the calling out, in *only* asking others' help, that night, the roots were twisted so that growth, trust in myself or perhaps some trust in fate, has lagged too far behind my fear. Too often I have sought (as we have lacked) some human help or "inner strength," and have not sought what fear most needs—(the silence of) in some sense, faith.

"Faith"—Jesse, is your Mommy *joking*?

Especially as I cannot express or know what, by words such as "faith" or "God," I'd mean. Yet—although my intellect, trained in philosophy, laughs "Put a thousand concepts, stretched to meaninglessness, completely contradictory, together, toss in 'existence,' and call this 'God'"—I still keep wondering could there even be meaning, substance, to this word.

There is, of course—and here is *no* argument, *no* proof "of God"—the awe. The sense of miracle before the newborn child, the knowledge that your dad and I were only vessels to your birth. The knowledge—terrible and basic—that the life and death is not in human hands. The fact there are the universe, the love, the blessings—and, again, the awe. But here words—*not* only because the intellect keeps laughing—have to fail; here, no speech, no meaning, can be possible. And where there is no meaning to a concept, then . . . .

Well yes, exactly.

Ah, and now you're laughing, too? With me, at me, in your sleep? See, Jesse, one cannot know, *cannot* speak of, everything, no way your Mommy can say, of this, what she means. Right now in fact she simply watches as your fingers twitch, mundanely; she merely shifts, like any animal, her legs, which have gone to sleep.

But if such issues seem abstract or mystic, far from my withdrawals or our daily needs, still they have for us real urgency. They are as urgent now as in the weeks of my decision—first to relinquish, then to raise you—when in dreams the seeking of supports slid in, replacing hope and what was sought, as if defending against deeper fear. The real issues are as urgent now as in those months I carried you and, though I called for help to doctors, therapists, and friends, the only honest voicing of my fear came when, in my bed, I lay in trembling silent tears which, acknowledging a helplessness, acknowledged helplessness only before whatever God, or destiny, or nothingness might be (or be conceived). And the urgency—urgent as our need for change—is this:

Faith, and courage, and what some call trust in people, in oneself, and in the world, cannot—just as they cannot be separated from the awe—be extricated from their opposites, despair and all the helpless acts of fear. It is precisely when what little I have found of faith or hope break that my soul most parts from you, and, as if myself a child beseeching "grown-ups," flail and voice those cutting cries. It is exactly at that point that, with my mind resounding "We must flee, but where? I *must now* give you up, and swiftly, if I'd save you," and reverberating to a too theatric inner voice repeating "Bye-bye, love, get used to it; bye-bye, you better get used to it," I—pulling back if you reach out, stepping away should you begin to cry, forcing my eyes once more to stare upon you as upon a stranger child—turn again into that other, evil Mommy you have known so well and long.

Last night, that is what happened. Such an instant, such a sudden crashing of any faith (of even our unspoken faith that other instants will succeed the present instant), was how last night's events began. It was itself both *what* occurred and why.

No, not quite why. We don't live in a den of quiet philosophy; any transcendent causes in our lives can only be *part* of what occurs, of "why." When last night the balance between hope and desperation tipped, it did so under the weight of every mundane stress, of every wearing, ordinary single parent family problem, that have piled on us through recent weeks—beneath *these* stresses which, night after night, have built:

The danger here, first, and the fear. The series of decisions by potential housemates not to move in after all. The isolation while our car was broken down, the lack of food and money after its repair. The social worker's warning that your daycare subsidy may soon run out. The fear of homelessness and ever present risk that our dependency on welfare may lead to foster care. As well as every other current fear and present danger, plus the weight of all we've been through and—no more important nor less ordinary than the rest—the resonations from your father's calls.

He first phoned—late (you were asleep), long distance—weeks ago, to say "I want to live with you and Jess; I *do* love you, I *do* love him; that is *our* baby, he is beautiful"—those words we'd heard last year—and then to add "I know I've told you all these things before, but I have thought, have *had* to think, about this, all alone here, every day. I have my conflicts—I have *had* to struggle with this—but now I know. Go tell that baby his Daddy's coming home."

Then, days after I'd told you—though hardly of his promise—of his words of love, he called to say (by then it was expected) "Yes, I meant it, but. . ."

And, phoning a third time—to inform me he didn't know when, if ever, he'd "return to that town but, in any case, this fantasy. . ."—he soon was speaking with such simple warmth (and you were hopping in such eagerness) that, in thoughtless spontaneity, I put you to the phone.

"Hi, Daddy. How're *you*, Daddy? Bye-bye, Daddy." I don't know what, or if, he replied.

But since those calls, no explanations ("Daddy loves

you but he can't come see us") have sufficed. Your first excited questions ("What my Daddy say, agin? When will *my* Daddy come?") have turned to groping queries about other children's fathers, spells of saadness, sporadic cries by night or day of "Daddy, come here, Daddy. Daddy, Daddy, *c'mere!*" I've had to see that, helpless as always before your father's cycles, I had allowed your hopes, like mine, to be raised high, then sharply be dashed down. And *this* remorse and disappointment weighed with all the rest in what occurred last night.

But what tipped finally the balance, so that in an instant courage, hope, and faith crumbled away, was not just this particular sadness or the sum of all our troubles but rather a minor, even trivial, catalyst.

We had just sat down to dinner when the phone rang. I went out into the hall to pick it up.

"I have decided"—it was a young woman who, quite friendly and compatible, had seemed inclined to share our house—"I need a safer neighborhood.

"Also, . . .well, I think I'd better tell you. There's—well, there is something there, there's something I cannot express but *feel,* some stress or tension in your home, that I could not . . ."

I placed the phone down when she'd finished, on the little table; I stood staring at the cracks along its case. I could not deny the truth in what she'd said, could not help remembering our most recent housemate's parting words, "Yeah, Jesse wakes me when he cries, but when you yell at him is worse." Angry or not, I could not deny my own guilt but had to look at the realities.

Meanwhile, you were still singing in the kitchen. Outside, the familiar silence of the evening had begun to fall. Warm, even fragrant, it would be, after so many weeks of fog and rain, the first clear starlit night of spring. The fragrance opened up my senses, like those of an animal relaxing from the tense preoccupations of the winter to the warming season's balm. I looked, eyes deep, across the room—and that was when I saw the silent closeness of our fragile windows. Acutely, suddenly, I became aware of what of invitation such a night must hold to those who prowl.

That was all. That was the whole, and just the start, of it. The first instantaneous collapse of normal trust, the first abrupt yawning of the void which, through the evening, would so often open to my sight. A minute later I—this Mommy who had brought the danger of our isolated nights here upon you—walked (eyes lowered to avoid all vision of those windows) back into the kitchen to rejoin you, sat down on her same chair by your side—and no doubt appeared, although no longer smiling, the very Mommy who, minutes earlier, had left the room.

You clapped—you *were* glad to have Mommy back. You went on singing. Happily, you reached out for a hug. Prepared to cuddle, offering me a spoonful of your food, you beamed; you leaned over toward me—not prepared at all for my response.

Sharply, I half-turned, I pushed your arm away. I leaned back further from you in my chair. I—who *could* not risk seeing your endangered joy—looked down, eyes nearly closed, away. I would, or could, not look up.

You paused, you made no sound. But—they are hardly new to you, my distances—after awhile you began again to sing. And, even as you realized your songs and laughter would not bring response, you simply sat back thoughtfully, sang another bar of song and tried just one more smile—and only very slowly, only as if forced back inch by inch, did you give in to recognition of my newer distance and take on—but very slowly, fighting it—the too-adult expression, halfway between pout and selfconsciously *attempted* smile, with which you might protect (or possibly deny) your feelings in the face of my suppression of both yours and mine.

Briefly, while I sat recalling that, just weeks before, you still were young enough you simply would have cried, you forced a teasing laugh. You laughed again, much louder. Then, in contrasting quiet, you tore to shreds the piece of toast upon your plate. Unmoving, eyes half-shut—and focused like my own upon the floor—you sat a moment, seeming (or was it guilt made me think so?) like a much older person struggling with some unvoiced question like "Why is my Mommy so unhappy? What is it *I've* done?" formed long before you knew the words. And then—confused, caught in shifting moods and trying to resolve their tension—slamming your hand down on the plate and kicking your chair with both feet, you lurched into one of your recent anxious build-ups, half-provocative, half-clinging, of intense activity as frantic and familiar as my own.

"Mom*my*!" Again, stentoriously, you raised your arm. In one swift arc, you swept your hand across your plate—and, striking your other fist (not very hard) against your cheek, you began to spill your remaining food, in handfuls, on the kitchen floor.

"*Bunny*"—you thrust your lower lip out—"*will* t'row beans down onna f'oor."

You had turned and squatted, facing me. "Now Mommy put yeg up onna chair. I wanna jump.

"Come awn. I wanna. Cm'*awn*.

"Dad*dy*!"

I still kept my eyes down, unmoving. Now you squeezed *your* eyes. Back and forth, you shook your head. You stood abruptly on your chair.

"I *will*"—you glanced across at me. "I *will*"—extremely carefully, you were pulling down your pants—"will too go pee-pee onna Mommy's kitchen f'oor.""

"Jesse—" But you had smiled; I had to smile back, too. And in some other mood, I would have been amused, delighted, by your readiness to challenge, recognizing your attempt to amuse, to tease response. But to smile back—to act on, thus to feel, my love—was to intensify the rising fear for you and risk reopening that gulf (between the love and fear, between what might have been and what we've known), and so instead, with what might yet seem normal, even calm, reaction to an ordinary "naughtiness,' I fixed you with a forced, intimidating stare while muttering "No, no," the threat lying only in the tone.

Which sufficed. You paused. And then—in a voice again clear and thoughtful, a tone as if just checking on a fact—"Mommy," you asked, "will spank bad Jesse?"

"*No.*"

No. But hadn't I spanked you when you'd wakened me the night before? "No, Jesse. Anyhow"—my words came out by rote—"Jesse isn't bad; Jesse is good."

"Mommy." For a moment, you sat locked in inner struggle; then searching carefully for the words, you brought out what, until this time, you had only expressed through tantrums, tears, or tearing up a favorite book. "No. No, Mommy." Again you spoke as if simply giving information. "No. I don't think so, no. I am not good."

Of the next half-hour, I remember only that I reached out to you silently, that I held you and reassured you, offering explanations, and that I was utterly uncertain whether you had given me a glimpse into what can become the most unshakeable and crippling of childhood secrets or were just acknowledging that no, it isn't good to pee-pee on the floor. Fearing the worst, and conscious it had taken this extreme to pull me back to you, I held you and I spoke, with no real expectations that mere words and gestures could much heal.

But—young, still open—you listened, quick to trust, perhaps to understand, possibly to believe—and quick, at my return of interest and tender voice, to tentatively smile.

"Yes, I are good. *Good* Jesse."

"Am."

"Yes, am, I am." You leaned against my shoulder, content.

For the next few minutes, chattering happily, you sat upon my lap. Soon, soothed, you cuddled against me, bemused and calm. I'd put my hand upon your shoulder; I was smiling at you and began to stroke your forehead—and it seemed we might get through the evening, somehow I could still contain the tension though it rose within. Then you reached out.

You lifted up your arms—you stretched out *both* your arms, you reached with both your hands, in an entire and instinctual act of love, the way small babies do—to touch my face.

And if tonight somebody should break in? The thought, in no way differing from my thoughts of every recent evening, crescendoed, in the reawakened tenderness, from fear for you to something close to terror. "*No!*"

"No, Jesse!"

Against the gulf—to fill the void that yearned from tenderness and therefore dread—I flung out words like rocks.

"No, you must never, never, never poke at people's faces, Jesse!" I pushed away your hands.

And then I started in to lecture you.

I found objection to your every action of the day; I took exception to each cry of every previous night. I reprimanded you for every move you made to draw me near; I scolded you for every smile or tear. I lectured on until you sobbed and couldn't eat—and then I lectured more, returning to our old, our overriding, theme.

"For three years, Jesse, for *three years*, you have, by your night-crying, made us move from place to place and chased out every housemate who's moved in. You've put us at the mercy of those with little mercy; you've put us in the mess we're in right now.

"Yes, *you*. And you have so much worn me out, so much exhausted me, have put me under so much pressure, that I have had no choice—*no choice*, you understand?—except to yell and scream at you.

"*Don't* smile! Why *should* you get attention? Listen,

"Just suppose—*suppose*—somebody finally does move in, suppose we find somehow another housemate; then. . . 'Wah-wah,' cries baby, '*Waah!*' What happens then? Or if noone moves in? *Where*—you just tell me where, just where—do you suggest we go?

"*Nowhere*." I laughed. "I'll tell you that. Nowhere, that's where. Not even shelters. Nowhere's where we can go. At least, while you still wake up everybody crying, any time of night—

"Hey!" I jumped up.

You had slid down swiftly from your chair. You ran into the living room.

I followed. You were climbing, seeking its familiar false security, onto our big stuffed chair. You had turned and, mouth set, eyes unwavering, were glaring back, confronting the lowering giant who, hands on hips, stood before you.

"Jess-ee." Admiration—and sheer shame to be casting

blame on you—stopped my onslaught only for a moment. Then, despairing but halfmeaning what I said, I went on, "Jesse—*do* you know what you need, Jesse? Another Mommy, that's what, a *rich* Mommy. And a Daddy, and a hundred other relatives so they could *spell* each other, and a *very* big house with your room at the end of a very long corridor . . . so you could cry and cry, and not wake anybody up, and we'd have *peace* at night." I stopped, unable to say more.

And silently I watched you. And it was as if the windows watched us—and beyond their glass there seemed to lurk some other truth. For the vision in my words had cut too close to our real needs and my old fear, the contrast with our lives too clearly lit our desolation. Briefly, only briefly, I could fling a screen, a silent song, (a song of parody, with words like "Get yourself another Maw/ You'll be better off, for shohr") against this stillness; then, although you had not heard my tune, your eyes filled up with tears (though mine dared not cry), and the void, the sadness at what could not be, opened wholly. "Jesse."

I repeated "Jesse. So." I stretched out my hands. "So, Jesse."

Slowly, I reached out. I gripped you, firmly but not harshly, by the upper arm.,

"So, Jesse, knowing what you need—" Gently I began to steer you past your toys, across the little rug, around the couch, toward our front door.

"—why don't you just—" My free hand fumbled with the latch—

"why don't you—" I was turning it.

"—go find them?

"Go ahead." I pushed you out. "Go find yourself another Mommy. Go on. Jesse, go."

Above, the stars were shining just as brightly as I'd feared.

You had neither said a word nor cried. You stood out in the darkness on the little porch; you didn't look back at me. My hands rose up to shut the door. But (I was shaking) even this small act took time. I had to keep my eyes from seeing you. I had to think—"It's warm out," "No one who'd hurt him is out there," "Another family, yes; yes, in the morning, I *will* phone the agency"—of other things.

And in that interval my mind, forced to the actions I refused my heart, took all the effort, the entire struggle through the desperation toward you, on itself. As if I'd opened up an ancient book, it raced in swift perusal through the wellworn causes of my fears and the despairs of our first years—the frightened first weeks and our two-months' parting and reunion, all the tensions and the harsh times and our isolation, the effects of both your father's early fears and mine—and the reality of danger to us here, as well as my habitual frightened awe before your innocence.

Then, skimming quickly over old analyses of my false, violent gestures of denial of my love, it took note once again that all the frantic self-anaesthetizing clamor struggles (as if crying "Someone ask what's really wrong here") to evoke—from some fancied audience of longgone housemates, crushing neighbors, distant "Daddy," and even prowlers in the night and that chimeric Caring Person (to whom *I* might call out "Mommy! Daddy!") yet anticipated at the mailbox or upon the phone—some gleam of help, security, or mercy, or at least cessation of all evil intent—struggles, above all, to hold off what in despair so often still seems our destiny: that I must lead you to—if not relinquishment—your ruin or your death.

"But when such a fate—" as if alone upon the mental page, the words leaped forth "—appears imposed by God, remember that any god one would *worship* loves."

I leaned—the whole time, I kept leaning—against the closed door. I wondered how, and *what*, my actions must seem to you. I thought "What if he cries? What if somebody—?" and of how little good self-analyses actually do. Yet, even as I shut and held the final latch, locking myself away from you as much as you from me, my mind, still seeking, turned up what appeared a novel thought—that, through my frantic gestures— as through my old attempts in our first homs to stop, by quieting your cries, our neighbors' clearly unrelated noise, or as through the constant bargaining of my rote prayers—I was attempting futilely to gain control of that which cannot be controlled, to take into myself and thus command what is beyond command—to turn, in short, our seemingly inevitable fate into mere farce, a *playlet* (far more tame than parody) where, as in your child's games or an ordinary fantasy, no harm is really done, no separation and no loss endure, and we might have once more a happy denoument.

This insight, in the way of insights, "looked good" only briefly. What might seem true tonight appeared far less true of the "bad nights" of our past, nor did my desperation *feel* like "act" or farce. Besides (my mind read on) there is a "natural history" of crazed and violent actions by all persons, from a schizophrenic child to whole oppressed minorities, whose simpler, clearer voice is crushed; not unrelatedly, my very "reversal"— seeking solace from the cold world while I coldly hold off you to whom I would give solace and love—comes also of entrapment in old conflicts of perception, in some early clash between "my" (every) mother's protective consciousness of an uncaring world and that world's "fatherly" rationality that doubts the "melodrama" in the mother's view. Moreover (it read on), there can be no doubt that *something* more than "trauma repetition" does still yield the never-completed cry "Give guarantees that I may raise him, or else take him, force me to give him up, that he be safe and whole." Further (should all of this be insufficient), it is a fact of common knowledge that most mammalian mothers may abandon, even eat, the young they cannot protect; and in any case, to understand the causes of an act does not . . .

Meanwhile, my hand had lifted. I was turning back both latches, opening up the door.

"Mommy." You had turned. You looked at me, your

eyes deep and serious. "Momm*ee*, guess what?" You pointed. "Pink yightbulbs *on* now! Pink yightbulbs be all right."

My arms reached out, as they had longed, across the fading void to hold you. I let you and reality back in.

The Prayer

Were her hands only free.

Dear Lord, I love You, amen amn. Drldlvymn amn mn.

It was nearly eight. Rochelle glanced again toward the clock. Ten minutes until her mother came in to awaken her. But she had to pray before she left for school. Not that she feared God; God is just.

Drldlvymn, mn. Dear Lord, Thou art just. Amen, mn.

It was right to pray every night, or in the morning if she fell asleep first. Probably right, that is; she could not really know unless she went to Sunday school to study Torah in the language of God's word. The Torah must be God's word, or why believe in Him?

Up the dungeon wall, straining in his chains, he hung.

His blood dripped down upon her hands chained behind her back.

It was too late to daydream.

Dear Lord, I love You, amen. Drldlvymn.

Dear Lord, I love You, and Thou art wonderful and merciful and great and kind and good and wonderful and the King of Israel and the Creator of Heaven and Earth, and I thank Thee for all the wonderful things Thou hast done—

Amen. Drldlvymn, amen.

The prayer must be begun again. She had looked correctly at the clear sky out the window before she closed her eyes, but it might have been streaked by clouds. It was necessary to see *nothing* before she prayed. Then would God know she tried to pray solely and unquestionably to Him alone.

Amen mn.

Six minutes to eight. If she did not pray, she couldn't get up for school. Her mother would stand in the doorway, fluttering her lashes and glaring from her wrinkled face.

And it wasn't wrong her mother be disgusted with her. She daydreamed when she went to bed, and didn't pray. She was "so afraid" to go to school, but never helped her parents around the house when they came home tired after work. She whined that kids at school didn't let her play with them, but how could they count on her when she was so often absent?

The first thing they had done was close the schools. And with the sweat fell blood.

Her parents mustn't know her daydreams. Her mother's eyes could flutter fury. Better if she told her mother of her prayers. But it would not be right to use her prayers for an excuse. She'd stayed home playing sick before she knew to pray. And to use her prayers for an excuse would not be to pray purely, to think to God.

Drldlvymn. Mn.

He was young and he hung in the chains. Gasping. Dying. The girl could not help him. If she were less thirsty, had they not whipped her all week. . . . He was hanging there. Just hanging and in pain. She could not help. "Oh, Bill," she whispered. Because they were Jews, they must be tortured and die, she and Bill and all their friends.

But she would get them out—scrape her thin hands from the twisting chains, squeeze through the narrow tunnel. . . . The girl looked around at their emaciated skulls, their bones chained on straw in their own excrement.

It was too close to eight. She had to think her prayers. She straightened her hair, unwound any spirals her fingers might have drawn, so that she could not be calling God crazy while she prayed.

Drldlvymn mn. Dear Lord, I love You, and Thou knowest I know Thou art not crazy. Amen. Amen.

She smoothed the sheet so it covered her flesh and fit up to her chin. God knew that she did not mean to offend Him, but He would also know if she did not try to pray purely. She clasped her hands so they rested over neither breasts nor stomach. Nothing must be felt nor seen nor heard; she was going to pray. Nothing must be thought of but God.

Not that God was a thing.

Drldlvymn, mn. Dear Lord, I love You, and Thou knowest that I know that Thou art not a thing, but that Thou art the one God, and I love Thee and thank Thee for all Thou hast done. Amen. Drldlvymn.

It was necessary to say more Amens than Dear Lords.

DrLord, Ilvymn. Dear Lord, I love You and Thou knowest I said Dear Lords meaning only the phrase as plural and that I know that Thou art one. Drldlvymn mn. She must do that whichwas right.

Two minutes before eight.

Drldlvymn. Mn.

Dear Lord, I love You, and Thou art wonderful and merciful and great and kind and good and wonderful and the King of Israel and the Creator of Heaven and Earth, and I thank Thee for all the wonderful things that Thou hast done for me and my family so far, and I thank Thee for granting me Judaism and freedom from fear and death and nuclear bombs and unhappiness—

—and I love Thee. Mn. Drldlvymn. Amn.

Someone had flushed the toilet. She could not pray when the toilet was being flushed, any more than when her parents made love. It was necessary to think only of God when she prayed.

It was eight, but there still might be time.

Drldlvymnmn. Dr Lrd, I love You, and Thou art wonderful and merciful and—mn. Mn mn. Amn.

"Rochelle, darling, time to get up."

Her mother's cigarette hung in her mouth. Her mother was tapping the doorjamb, wearing the bathrobe that smelled like being old.

DrldIlvymn. Mn.

The chains kept twisting her bloodied hands. "But I don't feel well, Ma." She must squeeze out of the chains and flee, or everyone would die.

"Rochelle dear, do you want breakfast first, or sleep?"

Drmn mn. Her hunger must wait until her prayers were thought.

She could not pray, here in the dungeon. Here, they lay in their excrement and suffering. Some, like Bill, hung from the wall. Somehow, she would save them—would flee on the black horses and find the refugees, lead them back to fight to save her people. "Bill, I love you," she whispered to the ragged, sweaty figure.

The Kickball Queen of Benjamin Smirch

After the rose-and-burgs and Herblock would have made her father and his friends lose their government jobs, and they all—she and Mom and Dad and little Moishie—been forced to move up to New York from Washington and live all cramped into one grimy room, hungry and snow-girt like the early immigrants, and after they would finally have moved out to the jagged mountains of the West, at last she would find a pure white stallion and, one day, a wounded murderer, deep in the steep rock gully, and they'd love. Or on a dusty afternoon, long after she had dared start Hebrew School to learn the Truth, she would have brought her parents and the other dark-haired fugitives into the wilds and tamed a great black mustang, and the famous cowboy on his palomino would ride beside her through the canyon, everyone be saved.

But anyway, somehow the tribulations over, and she grown strong from riding horses through the wild lands, she'd be back. Her parents would return them to the wood-and-brick red house in Washington and, for this final sixth-grade year at Smirch, she would—leg arched in glorious curve—prepare to aim her thin right foot in perfect home-run timing at the oncoming slippery ball.

She would be taller then, of course, her hair no longer black but gold. The boys would never call her "witch" or the girls sing "Shrimpboat's a-comin'" in the alleys walking home. It wouldn't be she who had to tag onto the other kids or get beat up, but rather she would say "Let's only beat up kidnappers and spies" and everyone would listen—and rush to crowd around her after every game.

No longer would they keep her off the field. She would be on the First Team, not the only substitute on Second or a special Third Team by herself. She wouldn't have to stand, where everyone could see, over by the Jungle Jim where little first- and second-graders played, during recess and before and after school.

And there'd be no more laughter when nobody else could answer Mrs. Knowhon's questions on the products of El Salvador or how many miles to the moon or what made national security. She wouldn't talk too fast the way her parents did and slur her words. She would know just what to say. And Mommy wouldn't have to drive the class on field trips anymore and have no life—for all the kids would want her for their mothers' cars and no longer choose her last like Maggie, who wore torn clothes.

Her parents might be happy then. Her mother would be soft and pretty, not skinny and sarcastic, and her father taut and thin-lipped, rifle slung across a shoulder; they would be young and handsome from the long days' riding and hunting like the pioneers.

And there, three cottonwoods sheltered the ancient trailer where they lived beside the rock-strewn creek, and halfway up the gorge a waterfall. And she'd have run away to join the Indians—only, not real Indians but outlaws— and have hid out once she'd met the murderer, becoming tough and brave. Only, first it would be necessary they lose everything and live in stench in the East Side Tenements, where she would study Torah and find right ways to pray. And also she would have to learn to ride a horse.

That would be hard.

Some weekends, if she hadn't stayed home playing sick, and if her parents had spare money for such luxuries and didn't think it too darn slippery outside, Daddy would give in finally and drive her to the stable north of Rock Creek Park.

The trouble was, she couldn't ride; she had trouble staying on the horse.

It was difficult to make one canter, or even trot, especially when it wanted to eat grass. The women who ran the stable put her on a plug for little kids without a fine touch on the reins. They put her up and made her use a switch—or, if she wouldn't, they switched the plug to make it go, and sometimes she'd fall off.

But things would be different afterward, even if the dumbclucks like the rose-and-burgs didn't cause an atomic war so there'd be only empty radioactive waste. It toughened man and woman, life upon the Range. Someday she would have galloped off with a really innocent murderer but then there would be tragedy—or maybe kids.

But eventually she'd have returned, her parents striding proud beside her, onto the playing fields of Washington; and it would be the climax of the playing season, the final kickball game.

The score would stand at 8–0 against Smirch that afternoon; each face would be tear-stained. Until at last she would come forth, fighting the kids' restraining hands that tried to hold her from the game. Fearless, blond, and sure of gait, she'd shove her lithe and ready body out upon the field of grit.

Her First Team satin shirt would gleam the blue and gold of Smirch. Her narrowed trailwise gaze would eye the bases, already loaded, the speeding, onrushing sphere. Her rock-hard leg would poise, arched in perfect form. Then she would kick.

And the globe, lifted upward, would arc high and higher, a big, bright, crystal jewel against the winter, fall, springtime blue sky. Her first home run.

And only she would kick, and only kick home runs.

Until at last the people would come running toward her, chanting, singing, hands outstretched—the kids and teachers, her parents and her brother Bobby, even Gordon who'd only liked Maria—waving pom-poms, lifting banners, flinging kisses, chanting. And the anthem would be playing, flags unfurling—white stars, red stripes, blue—while the green and gold and pink and purples would gleam brilliant in the sunshine, cheering finally the one true kickball queen.

Smirch would just have won its most important game.

Or would have—except, climbing the steps up to the dais to accept, for Smirch, the purple Victory Ball from Roosevelt Elementary, she saw little Sue, Roosevelt's substitute shortstop, sobbing, surrounded by their team's best players, who were chanting "Fumble-dumble Suzie, Suzie made us losie," and she felt like crying like dumbie Sue—or maybe hugging her, which was weird—so she looked at her toes instead so no one could see and tossed the Victory Ball down on the grass.

Berkington

I finally went out. Today in the heat, I went with Mother to the store. We stayed, I think, half an hour. Mother bought a nightie—other things too, enough I had to help carry the bundle from the car, but I don't know what was in it, I don't care to know; we were out half an hour. When I am out, I realize I am here in Berkington again. I have to see this city, the color of its air, to smell its air, its heat; and the air smells of Berkington, the trees of Berkington. Today we went shopping; I am back; I must realize I am in Berkington again. Also, something is wrong with the car, and I am scared.

There is no escape out of Berkington. I have been broken down and been returned, bad merchandise, to Berkington; this has happened before. All I do is lie on the bed. Rock myself and listen to the radio. Mother and Father sit downstairs and watch the television, bored. I close out their voices, try to close the war cries from the television.

This evening I read the news. It is worse. They say that China has much larger bombs than we are told to think. I know some wish to drop this country's bombs, or use the germs, before the Chinese may. I do have reason to be scared.

I took a second shower. I must stay clean, for when the germs or bombs fall. The danger is in each of us, yet there is danger outside, too.

Mother said, "Go out. Take a walk, but not the car." I threw an ashtray but I missed her. This is as it used to be. I will hold up, rock me to sleep, pretend—shall dream—that I am not in Berkington. Yet this is how it was in Berkington before, when I first broke in Idyllca and was returned as if to rightful owners. Only, now, far after child-times, I'm again returned to Berkington. Where Mother, Father still watch television, downstairs in the living room, still bored, each with the other, still don't quite know what to do and how to make time stop, to make oncoming age, death stop, their life not flop. It is too dark, the lights too dim. In Berkington, lights are, now as before too dim to read; only, now, the paint is duller, the walls in the kitchen brown from grease, the windows tight-stuck, the air turned hotter, sky more pink; it grows harder to breathe. The rooms have shrunk, the curtains stringy on the bottom edges; the mirrors greened, too dusty to reflect the night. Again I've been returned to Berkington, and there is nothing left.

Mother came upstairs again. She leaned around the door, but withdrew too fast—I missed. What she wanted was to say, "Go outside." Outside is Berkington; I do not go outside.

In Berkington, they riot on these nights. I think, "If I were younger, I could join them," but could this be true? I have been returned, and the car has stopped. I am afraid; outside is Berkington. And they are rioting. They drive in the streets, in these times, by night in fast cars.

Yet even in the blackout, outside the Whitehouse, struggling by the thick miasmal river, they are walking and they picket and they protes; but do they understand the world as you or I? They are rioting, screaming, are dangerous, I'm told—though what they say is "Bombs kill! Peace."

The Net says China has too many bombs and novel germs. The pundits say that China is too close and does not care what's done, that China might or might not use its missiles, rain its missiles down on Berkington. They do not say about a germ or whether bombs will fall here if this country's bombs hit China. They say all is well, "It's fine."

In the blackout, there is shouting. Were I younger, I could join them. Only, I was younger once, when I had broken down in Idyllca and been returned to Berkington.

It is 99 degrees today; the humidity is 99 percent. I tried to go swimming. I thought that I would walk down to the bus—could make myself walk down the street, full knowing that I was in Berkington, and take what bus still runs out to the swimming pool; I thought I could go swimming, make myself put on a bathing suit, here in this house in Berkington, and walk along the street to take a bus to the pool in Berkington, to swim in the pool.

I did not go. I did not put on my bathing suit. I have taken three showers today and I've cried—or not, only lain in silence—but no imagining has worked, and, though I've dreamed of flowers, "cried as in the wilderness," peeked into silence, still I am in Berkington; I was sent back as if my job here was to die.

Mother said, "Have lunch. What shall I fix?" but I ignored her. I may have cancer—or a heart condition, AIDS, blood poisoning; I may be dying. I may never get back to Idyllca.

To Idyllca. Oh, Idyllca! The people are in Idyllca.

It is my own fault. I wanted Idyllca too much—to stay in Idyllca, its forests and those flowered meadows and bright lakes, be loved there by the people and to love the people. Yet I knew that if I tried too hard, that if I were not altruistic, kind, that if I could not fight—that if I could not fight, be witty, quick, be bright and light enough to bring the people to my side—that I would break and be returned. Yet, knowing, still I did not stop, but cut my life too easily—that is, I did not fight the right way, there in Idylca—and I have been returned to Berkington to die.

It was 104 degrees this afternoon in Berkingon, inside. I rocked me and then dreamed. I dreamed about a man some called a prophet; he stood with two wolves on the ice. He stood on Ice Mountain on the far side of the globe. The people crowded on this beachball nodded. "Nothing can be changed," the prophet said; "There is no hope." The people crowded in the lifeboat didn't answer; they watched the news, they watched each other, knew that they were doomed, there was not room for everyone. They knew some would—it was a certainty—be superceded soon. They said they all felt well. The prophet made the orange roll away. I started to object, they would fall off, but he was sad; I saw his eyes were sad and felt he too had been in Idyllca, though I'd not known him there. He saw I understood he sorrowed that we nodded at our doom. "The prophecy fulfills itself," he said, "when those within believe it." He laughed; I realized I must not accept his words as certain either. I knew that, if I had not fought in Idyllca, that if I'd been like moldy merchandise returned, that if I'd not been altruistic, brave—still I may fight though I have been returned to die.

They pushed me off the beachball. There were others with me, and we struggled in the river; we swam through thick green algae in the river; I peered out across the road. The people on the sidewalk didn't see me; they'd been shopping and knew nothing of the bombs. They carried bundles; Mother moved among them, Father too. He held his briefcase; he was with the men returning home from work. I tried to warn them of the germs, but they'd their phones up and didn't hear. Somebody said the rioters were dangerous, filling up the road.

A black-bandanaed rioter started toward me, and I warned him if they filled the road, there'd be no room. Too hot in Berkington.

Yet they were on my side. I felt my hand take something, grip—the wooden picket sign. I knew it was a stupid thing to do. The Whitehouse troops attacked the rioters. I thought, "I have survived myself; now help this people"—this person, rather, for the man in the bandana fell—"or else it is too late." I thought to help this person—people—but these rioters were crowding up the road, had done a stupid thing to do. I knew that someone would be hurt; they couldn't want me on their side. And I had never fought in Idyllca, was not kind, altruistic, brave. I knew it was too late. I saw their feet might crush the rioter; I knew I had to help or die. I'd been returned and there would be no other time.

I'd lose all that I had if I must leave it by the river road, and I was late. A second chance would do, but soon they'd turn the lights off, all become unreal, and I'd not fought, my feet were cold, I'd not gone swimming though I could. Only now was the second chance. To fight beside the man with the bandana—else, the wolf must put me in a bottle in the battle in the ice: "Bye-bye; you had a dream."

Tonight again I went downstairs. I had been peeking

54

through the window at the trees, pretending they were not the trees of Berkington, and listening to the fast cars, all the rioting outside. I could not see the riots by the Whitehouse, southeast, near the river, at Ground Zero. I have heard people scream, heard people cry "Peace now!" downtown, outside. One can't escape from Berkington, too dangerous outside in these times; just bolt the door, stay where you're kept, to die.

Mother and Father said the car was stopped. Outside was silence—no voices, no television. In the blackout, dark inside as on the streets. I looked first in the downstairs closet. Upstairs, my cloak hung in my mother's closet, frayed. It had got frayed in Idyllca, those days before I broke and was returned to Berkington. I rustled newsprint, squeezed my hands, stared at my cloak.

It was hanging from two hooks. Mother must have put it there, on two hooks, that way. Silent, I stood in the dark house; outside was dangerous and they'd said the car was stopped; to try might kill me. I might never, now, return to Idyllca, had been returned to Berkington to die. The bombs might fall at any time, the germs escape; the rioters, the roads, might kill; somebody could be hurt, be killed—no second chance.

Unless . . .

Reaching out, I lift my cloak from each hook, wrap the cloak around me, run downstairs. Fearing to lift the screen-door lock and turn the Golden Safety Knob, I peer outside. A car drives silently between the house and sidewalk, crushes down the grass. They are driving across the lawns now! In cars now turned strange; a white car drives across in silence—kidney-shaped, with seats for only three.

I may never get back to Idyllca. My fault—the guilt, the shame are in me too. I've been returned—the people returned me. I feel the heat of Berkington; I know the danger in these times, have read the news online. It is much worse; the germs breed, and the Chinese, as we heard in Idyllca, have more bombs than we're taught to think. Heat rises; someone soon will bomb an "other side."

I was afraid, I could not fight, I feared. I was returned to Berkington to die—

Unless I take a step outside and go out on the road to reach the demonstrator lifting, though fallen, his picket sign.

A mirage of a small man comes from behind the parents' car and says "I'll keep you safe" to guide me back inside, but I ignore him, though I'd heard the shames were in me too and people out there had no need of me, might use me, and I must stay in and keep the rioting outside the Golden Safety Grate, put back the cloak on two hooks.

Only, the man in the bandana is reaching out his hand—

Before me, through the wavering dawn, all prophets on the ice now vanish. I see, hear, and—although I was returned to Berkington to die and have had reason to be scared, and though germs multiply and bombs will fall— I run out in the rising light to raise, with this demonstrator, the fallen protest sign.

Our hands reach, strive to shade these people all around, though germs may leap and bombs may fall.

But in the blackout, sirens have begun to sing.

Days of Changes—Theme, Variations, and Reprise

Petit récit d'une maquisarde

(traduccion anglaise 2003,
Térèse Marie-Claire Marlemovitz)

Not knowing who you are who may encounter these words of a woman so agèd, I do not know, messieurs'-m'dames, if you will understand.

Watching you young people, shabby longlegged creatures marching or else begging on the streets, I think it is for you hard times as for us long ago, those days called "World War II." So that you cry for peace as we would whisper—we dared not publicly proclaim—our own first challenge to the state. Oh yes, you have seen films, read books, you surf your Net, you know how few took actions, even as now. How few—especially sadly in my country, its long pretensions of egalité, of liberté so quickly cowed—ran the great risks.

We who did were not very like you in our hopes. Today

your challenges extend beyond the political or economic worlds. The structures to hold off a rising ocean, new diseases, encroaching heat—of these, we'd little need. Of how to dress, new ways to think, new ways to be toward one another "in community," all forming a living unity: to us this could only have seemed absurd or as some distant luxury.

In Lyons I had achieved, you see, very high notice in my studies. This was no surprise to my parents. Probably soon, despite the hard times, the nice classmate who used to ride his bicycle beside me would ask for my hand. Exactly what would follow was somewhat vague; up in Paris *liaisons* might make up normalcy, but the boundaries of questions and moeurs were much restricted in what you, here, would call "the sticks." Of course we condemned our government—too soon the Vichy gang, Lavalle, those pigs; how could we not? Only, you see, because everything was very difficult, there was no time and we never thought beyond our urgent anti-Fascist struggle; certainly we did not think, for example, to go beyond our too-provincial notions of what ought not to happen except between husband and wife.

So when, there by the railroad crossing on the darkening hillside by the little road that came out from the forest, how could I have joined Jean-Tomàs? In that moment when we saw the train—this train you understand so full of prisoners locked into cars—and Jean-Tomàs leapt forward in the shadows, how could I? When he so bravely, planning already to swing around and—like a thin gazelle, you see—run up the slope to come out far from us, on the opposite side of those tracks, protecting us, how could I have dared to join him? How could I—even had I, so pregnant, raced fast enough, in that so suicidal attempt—join him? To be with him then, or since?

Because, though we had been lovers briefly, there in the Maquis in the urgency of those times, never had there been an indication he would marry me, and so to have raced forward with him must have claimed—proclaimed . . . what I *must not*, do you see? Do you comprehend? Can you understand that to be lovers had some property, to someone of my circumstance and time, of shame? To have gone forth in that singular surety of suicide with Jean-Tomàs would have appeared to claim as mine, and perhaps thus to embarrass, him—and at such a moment, messieurs, m'dames! So. While of course another part of me said, also, "This is not the only way you will harm him. You will endanger his life—and your baby's too— should you run out there; you will bring down these comrades, will be seen." These last, you may be sure, may have been true.

By now you've imagined what happened to Jean-Tomàs, yes? Through some miracle he was not shot down, he placed the explosive at the curve, the engine was derailed. And he—and two comrades who, ignoring fear, raced forth with him—broke open three of the cars so that, before the Fascists regained control, fifty people did escape.

Then we all scattered from one another deep into the

countryside for many days.

Jean-Tomàs never knew, I think, though he tried, how I felt about that event; he took my feelings for something different, saying "You were pregnant, I am glad you were afraid." Even before this, we were distanced, and in our circumstances we had no leisure to discuss these matters, even were a man and woman to so incline. But he would say he needed my love, and with this I became sure I was fully woman, and began to grow past my sticky shames. The guilt, as well—I saw that en verité to stay with the person you love, no matter what, is simply to do *the good, to do what we long to*, and I knew I would go forth the next such time.

And I did. In the fight by the coule d'argent, the silver creek.

But subsequently the repression worsened. Comrades had been denounced; many were killed, others forced to flee. Jean-Tomàs and I had no further chance to create what might have been. His group was sent into the mountains. In my growing pregnancy, and after we heard Jean-Tomàs had been taken, I was removed to a supposed "safe house." Perhaps it would have been.

Dear friends, I do not know what would have happened. And perhaps I could have cleared away misbeliefs, dared to not yield (as then was the habitude) for adoption my "out of wedlock" baby. Such a difficult jump this would have been, even for what you call, with heroics, a "resistance fighter"; this was not as now in your day, not even as in your parents'. So that . . . no, I would have yielded him—had to yield him—away, the tiny one beside me on the great straw mattress beneath the attic roof, the sweet small baby with his huge eyes following mine. I would have believed this necessary.

But then the safe house turned out not to be, and in prison, one terrified day we awaited our train's departure, they took him. Only years later I learned he had not been sent separately, but given to a couple somewhere to the north.

Of course, one does never forget, but now in my old age it is like someone seeking me. Unforgotten, even now when none know what will happen to us in our failing hospitals, these millions sickened, and soon worldwide what is to come. I do not know who you are, hearing this; will you comprehend?

The Man in the Creek

It was coming into the full moon, that early summer evening—blistering heat after too cold a winter, anti-Vietnam-War protests downtown near the White House, rumors of another murder in Bethesda—when young Mara Bernovski turned the stallion for the first time toward a red-clay gully at the northern edge of Rock Creek Park.

Ears back, Stormy reared, his forelegs stiff. She let him plunge, her long hair flopping, and struggled to stay balanced. Urging him sharply forward, she sat bolt upright as she'd seen the stable manager, Gerilee, do a hundred times, and, hands gentle but steady on the reins, guided him along an overgrown game trail, down into the steepening gully. The horse no longer balked; he was nearly to the bottom, almost to the water—indeed, his left foreleg had already stepped into the turgid current—when he glanced to his left and once more reared.

"Stop it!" Nearly thrown, Mara flung herself against the gleaming neck. "Down—there's nothing scary here." But at that moment she saw the form.

Black hair grimed by mud and water, covered with dirt and blood, a man lay half-hidden behind the vines and granite rocks. He barely seemed to breathe. Blood was caked along his torn, green-and-blue striped sleeves and down across one thigh, his hands spread flat against the clay, and his legs lay helpless in the shallow current. Shivering, badly injured—but nobody ever came here, and this person was haggard, filthy. He must be someone desperate—crazy maybe, or even a criminal, maybe the Bethesda murderer. Her eyes caught the pallor under the olive skin, the foreign hollowness of the narrow cheeks. Could be that bomber who'd blown up the soldiers and the woman passer-by, downtown.

The horse rose higher, kicking out. The man moaned, frightened or in pain. Whoever he was, he couldn't move and he didn't look much bigger than she was. Eyes fixed on his face, she jerked the reins so Stormy's forelegs landed to one side.

"Whoa." Her voice tried to stay firm, but her whole body trembled. "It's okay, I'm here." But no, she should turn the horse's head right now, and flee—for once remember her mother's warning, *It's risky for a girl, out in those woods.*

With a sighing sound, the man turned his eyes and looked up. It seemed difficult for him. Black eyes, intelligent.

A cool breeze stirred the oaks. Stormy snorted. Shifting her weight, Mara swung her right leg cautiously over the saddle.

The man kept trying to focus on her. He must be twenty-two, twenty-three, even older. *You've more brains than this*, she told herself, hopping to the ground. Besides, it was time to get the horse back to the stable. Gripping the reins, she squatted down. "Can you talk?"

The pale lips barely opened. She barely caught a word, something like "so" or "don't." But when she started to lean closer, her hair nearly touched that filthy body. "Can't you say what's wrong?" she asked, and hesitated. "Yeah, I better go get someone to come help."

Flinging up a hand, the man jerked; a sort of spasm shook his chest and head.

"Someone who can really help you," she added.

His blood was spreading on the ground; his hands clawed at the earth. The afternoon that the Haradays' cat had got hit by a truck and she had tried to save it, it had clawed and clawed in that same way.

"All right. All right then, I won't go. You can stay here." She didn't mean it as a promise.

The eyes searched for her, maybe gratefully. Then they closed. A black fly buzzed across his face. As if he had just died.

She lurched back toward Stormy. Petting the thick

mane, she watched the man's prone figure, trying to see his chest move. Then she heard a harsh, rasping sound as he took a breath.

But how could she keep someone breathing? If only she'd paid attention during First Aid class. He was doing okay, though, staccato but a regular rhythm—no need to touch the grimy chest. Just check for bleeding and . . . she couldn't remember the rest. Along the man's left arm, under the twisted shreds of sleeve, a blotchy area surrounded a deep-looking round hole—like pictures of a bullet wound. It looked so real.

"This has got to be cleaned." *Don't let him see I'm scared.* "Let's get you on dry land, first." Forcing herself to grab the sticky shoulders, she began to pull him up the bank. But it was almost impossible, and when she slipped and let go, he groaned, a sound he stifled but that made her want to hide. Leaning against the red-clay slope, she braced her feet against the trunk of a thick old forsythia and struggled, slowly so as not to hurt him, dragging him from the creek.

"Okay," she breathed at last. "Okay."

For the clay shelf here, though rough, seemed nearly dry; an almost solid line of brush and vines and one high boulder screened him from the path, and the overhanging bank gave a bit of shelter. But those gaping wounds still had to be cleaned, which meant touching him again—and he stank, not only with sweat.

And he could be somebody deadly, despite those eyes. Again she took a step back toward the horse.

Long ago, someone in Europe had rescued Mom and Granma from the Nazis; some things, one just did. Patting Stormy, she jerked open the saddlepack, pulled out the emergency kit that Gerilee made every horse trainer carry. She turned. "Wake up," she urged the man. "Please."

His eyes opened. "Go on, miss." Nearly too weak to hear, his voice was polite, precise.

Only, I don't know what to do.

But she had to. At least, he didn't cry out when she washed the wounds and put on the iodine and covered them with gauze—the bullet hole or whatever it was, and that raw mess along the outside of one thigh, skin mixed with blood and shreds torn from his jeans. His skeletal face just stared, with an empty look that wasn't only pain. And when she asked him to turn his left arm so she could clean the wound there, he was too weak. He kept on shivering, so she untied her windbreaker from behind the saddle and stretched it across his chest. Then she remembered her wool scarf—Mom was always bugging her, "Carry something warm, dear, just in case."

As she lifted the scarf from the pack, Stormy whinnied. Past the thick trees, the woods were turning dark; people would be getting upset, back at the stable. She stroked the horse's muzzle. If they came looking for her, they would find this man, and he must be a fugitive of some kind, the way he'd panicked—maybe not a murderer, or even the People's Liberating whatever-it-was bomber, but somebody in hiding. Could be a draft dodger—he was no foreigner, from his voice. "I need to go soon," she said.

But if she left, he could die.

His lips, so pale they looked white, moved in a half-twitch. His words—which might have been "And so?" but sounded more like "absurd"—were followed by a choking sigh. It made her want to pat him, to tell him he'd soon be strong again.

"I have to take the horse back now," she said. "Otherwise they may come searching." She wasn't sure he understood. "Here"—she pulled the windbreaker tight around him, wrapping the scarf so it covered the back of his head—"stay warm." She placed the half-full canteen beside his right hand, along with a box of crackers, the only food in her saddlebag. Pulling off his waterlogged shoes and socks, she covered his feet with her new issue of *Horse & Saddle* and a pile of crinkled leaves. He had stopped shivering, but what if the night turned cold?

"My Mom will be picking me up soon," she said. "She may be at the stable already, she gets frantic fast. I'll come back tomorrow—if I can." She didn't know what else to say. He just kept staring, eyes glittery.

"I will," she said. Then, hurriedly, she untied Stormy's reins. Like someone crossing slippery ice, she began to back up, caught now by that stare that seemed to follow her every motion—until, beyond the shrubbery, she turned and, stepping carefully, led the stallion up the gully path.

For the first time since she'd climbed down from the saddle, fear took over; she almost wet her pants. The game path was already dark, oaks and maples crowded close, though the sky still glowed with light. Stormy pranced, ears stiff, prepared to bolt when she tried to mount. The bomber, people said, was insane—and dangerous crazy people lurking in the park's thick woods had been her parents' biggest argument against the riding job.

Gerilee came marching from the stable office. "Hey, a *job* means getting back on time, gitl. And paying attention where you ride. You pull this again, no more Stormy days for you here. Get it?"

Mara nodded, head bowed, clasping the damp reins tightly and shaking in her wet clothes. It had seemed a brilliant inspiration—ride Stormy into Rock Creek, slide off, pretend she was late because she'd been too busy looking at the rising moon and fallen in. No, a dumb idea—Gerilee knew very well she didn't go tumbling off horses anymore. And Gerilee had trusted her.

"Yeah, and that five-dollar emergency kit? You couldn't remember to strap shut your saddlepack?" The stable manager's deep voice laughed, but her eyes were hard. She tossed a mended bridle up over the doorframe. "I mean, you know better, Mara." Again the deep laugh. "Well, never mind—this once, we'll let it go. I guess we all fall off sometime. But no more—you all right on that?"

It was the same thing Gerilee had said back in May, hiring her to exercise the stallion. "Let him race himself out to his heart's content—you all right on that? That's a mustang, girl, a rebel like me." They had been soaping saddles in the tackroom, under the horseshow trophies and the psychedelic poster of a dove with giant claws. "You run that horse three times a week—more, if you work out. And you will. You're not the timid crybaby folks think." Now, slouched against the wall, Gerilee finally smiled. "Remember when you were half the size of all the other little squirts and you'd tumble off of every horse we tried? Even Layover?"

Mara nodded. She'd never forget, or how much it had mattered—horses, riding, all that. "Even Misty." She smiled back. Glad to, glad to be here. Here in the warm. Here in reality. With the stable manager and Stormy— and even Mom, who was coming slowly toward them, stepping awkwardly across the littered yard in her "down-town" office shoes and narrow skirt.

To be here—not worrying about that person, who could be very dangerous.

Who might be dead by tomorrow. What if she went back to find crows eating those eyes?

"Mom, I need to get home." She struggled to keep her voice low and calm, to speak the way somebody college-bound, somebody nearly seventeen who wasn't hiding secrets, would. "Mom, let's get home fast, please? So I can dry off? And then tomorrow I'll ride Stormy really care-fully." She turned to Gerilee. "If I may? I'll do it extra."

Gerilee tossed her dark curls, standing proud the way she must have in her Freedom Rider days. "I don't know why not, Mara. We want to see you succeed."

"Indeed." Her mom, lighting a cigarette, breathed out smoke. "Actually, Miss Tassevara, I am very happy for this chance to thank you. This is the first real interest Mara has stuck with, since when." The smile was fake. "Whenever," Mom corrected herself.

The stable manager's eyes went wide. Gerilee knew about horses and teaching riding, but she didn't understand Mom, what Mom had gone through back in Europe, how fast she got upset. Gerilee was saying, "She seems a pretty on-top kid to me, Mrs. Bernovski. She's got"—stressing the word—"smarts."

Mom must be furious; she just blew a second long puff from her nose. "Brains, yes. But when it comes to persidurance"—it was embarrassing, Mom still mixed up words—"not so much. Mind may be enough, back in Poland or someplace. But not here."

"That so?" The stable manager was putting on a client-helping smile. "That little girl used to scarcely say 'Boo,' and now she's into every nook and cranny. You know she's got all our trails by heart?"

But Gerilee couldn't see that Mom was hurting. Though it wasn't clear what got to Mom; sometimes she acted totally alone.

Like that man in the woods, who'd maybe said "absurd." He needed help, but he had clawed the ground like the Haradays' cat to get away.

At least the night had not been cold. Only the humid swampiness of Washington, and now the morning was thick with miasmic heat as she rode the bus to Chevy Chase and then another down the Beltway to the road beside the stables. Stashing the shopping bag near Upper Meadow, she rested briefly, swatting at mosquitoes. The bag held a blanket and her waterproof poncho from riding camp, first-aid supplies, scissors, water—all she could carry—and penicillin from her mother's downstairs "just-in-case" drawer.

Walking toward the stable, she pulled change from the pocket of her bell-bottoms—enough for the bus home. In the white-shingled barn, all the horses were in their stalls, except Misty and two mares. The stable manager was out—"teaching the littles," said Eric, the old groom. Stormy fought when she tried to saddle him, but soon she was up on his back and, striking the path to Upper Meadow, she stopped to gather her stashed supplies, then forced him to a trot, then quickly to a canter, startling an oriole from the grass. Stifling hot here, already the horse was sweated up, but she *had* to hurry. She must help that person—if he still was alive.

Two miles farther on, she curved from Western Trail onto the overgrown game path and, letting Stormy find his own careful footing, urged him downward toward the gully.

Everything was silent; vines on the clay banks hung in the windless air. She leaned far forward in the saddle, searching. There were the screening bushes; there was the dark overhang with its shielding, trailing vines, that heap of rocks, the largest like a boulder. And, beyond, the man—lying exactly as she had left him, her windbreaker to his chin, scarf loose about his head, canteen untouched beside him though his lips looked cracked and dry. But still living—she made out his chest moving. The black eyes might even see her, though she couldn't tell. What must the night have been for him?

Afraid Stormy would bolt, she lashed the reins around a dogwood and dragged down the supplies. She thought again of Sonja hiding Mom and Granma in her attic, daring to help people no matter what. Kneeling by the man, she lifted the jacket, began to wash his wounds; they didn't seem much better—maybe a bit less red. She stared hard for a minute, then, working up the courage, cut away his clothes and carefully cleaned the filth from his skin. But the odor was nauseating, and after she finished she sat on a flat rock upstream, taking long breaths. The man began shivering again, though; quickly, she dressed his wounds and spread the blanket over his chest.

Then she fit a straw into a juice can and, helping him raise his head, placed the other end to his lips. He only sighed, as if unable to try anymore.

"Come on," she urged, "you can." A drop or two ran into his mouth, and she heard him swallow. He took three more swallows before his head rolled back against her arm.

"Well, that's all right." It was as if he were Stormy—or her little sister, Hannah, when Hannah was very young. She wanted him to be all right, to get better. He was sleeping.

A mockingbird started up nearby. She listened, but no one came near. Stormy stared resignedly into space, only snorting at an occasional small animal—a squirrel or frog—in the brush. An hour passed, maybe two. She sat still, trying to recognize bird calls, holding this stranger against her aching upper arm, wondering why she did it, and giving warmth that might save his life.

About three o'clock, a shaft of sun came directly through the trees onto his eyelids, and they opened. She started. The eyes looked darker—softer, more alive.

"You *held* me?" His voice was again precise. She squeezed his arm, to say *You'll be all right*, but his lips moved and he asked, though barely audibly, "This whole time?"

He must be confused. "Just this afternoon." Again she added, "You do need a doctor, you know. Don't bullets have to come out?"

He didn't act frantic this time, only sad. "They went through," he breathed, as if at something silly. "Through *me.*"

It was late the next afternoon before she could get back to Park Northern Stables. She rode into the gully to find the man unconscious, and it was only by coaxing juice and water from a straw into his mouth—until he would convulsively, and as if unwillingly and from a far distance, swallow—that she could get liquids into him at all.

The next day, she told her parents she was spending the afternoon with her friend Nina, whom they trusted. Traveling on foot from the bus stop, staying far from the stable to avoid being sighted, she came again to the gully and sat for another two hours, sometimes humming a song the way Mom used to when she or Hannah was sick with flu, beside the silent form that seemed to hover halfway out of life.

At the breakfast table the next morning, her mother was suspicious when Mara said, "I'm going downtown today, to the National."

"Why is that, dear?" The words came around a cigarette.

"To the National *Gallery*. Why do you think?" Mom's probing could get extreme. Still, it was awful to lie.

"I didn't know you were 'into' art." Mom put a Mendelssohn recording on the stereo and started revving up the sarcasm. "Perhaps you will come to the Frick sometime when I am curating. Or this is something new from Nina? I hadn't heard."

Why should it matter who something came from? "There's lots," Mara snapped, "you haven't heard." But that was too true. She cut an orange into wedges and lifted two slices of bread from the toaster.

Her mother lit another cigarette. "Have it your way, darling."

"Mom, you want some toast?" She held out hers; she had scarcely begun to butter it. She hated it when Mom looked at her patiently this way, like waiting for disaster.

When finally she reached the gully, two hours later, the

man was no better. Though he seemed to hear when she tried to sing, and drank on his own after she put the straw between his lips, he made no sound when she cleaned the wounds, and he didn't seem to see anything, the few times his eyes opened, at all.

That night, she couldn't read, but kept having to stop herself from running downstairs to tell Mom, "It's because somebody hid you and Granma from the Nazis." Dad would agree, "She's got a point there, Beyla," and they'd all get in the car and bring the person home, into the safe, dry house.

Except, *Don't be an idiot*; this was just thinking like a child. What Mom would do was get cold furious and snap "You make comparisons?" and look a hundred years old. And Dad would call the police, and later, half-joking the way he did, say, "This isn't one of your little stray kittens or injured robins, Bubbie. What you need is a bit of horse sense." There would be sirens, men racing into the gully with guns.

Only, without help, a person hurt so badly could die. Even this moment. Even if the man was the suspect. No, any moment. . . . Pushing up from her desk so fast she banged her knee, she ran to the window, pressed her nose against the damp screen. Only four blocks to Connecticut Avenue, but the Beltway Express didn't run after ten at night. In the pink darkness, rain drizzled steadily.

She smiled so hard she could feel it, the corners of her mouth pushing up her cheeks, to see him glance up quickly, hearing her and Stormy. He half-leaned on an elbow on the blanket, a juice container empty at his side. He was watching her with a terribly intelligent look.

Seeing her windbreaker draped across those dirty shoulders, she felt her stomach lurch with fright. But the man could barely move. Unless by now he was just faking; it was five days since she'd found him. On the news, they said a suspect had been caught in the Bethesda murders but the terror-bomber remained loose and dangerous. He had fled into the woods, they said. But that had happened miles away, down where the park road went beneath the Calvert Bridge.

"Who are you?" she started to ask, but he spoke first.

"Why are you helping me?" His voice was weak.

"Because"—she said the first thing she thought—"you're hurt."

"You're . . ." A sort of tremor went over him, and the weakness sucked him down so he fell back and lay flat on the blanket.

"I'm what?"

He just lay there. Finally he said, "You're not afraid?"

She didn't answer. The police had said the bomber belonged to a little-known group called People's Liberation Tribe, and was not only dangerous but insane.

"Does your, does your"—it took him a minute to finish, as if he'd forgotten something—"your mother know you're here?" He seemed to smile, but not at her. Maybe he was just glad someone was there. But it made no sense. Too quickly, she washed his wounds and placed the gauze and iodine at his side. She shoved the penicillin bottle closer. "To stop infection," she said. She felt embarrassed, scaring so easily—this was part of what she had to change. "You take those pills."

He didn't answer, just stared. Everything was where he could reach it himself, but really she wasn't sure he was strong enough to.

On the television news, the FBI man said, "We have new evidence linking the Flag Day bomber"—or some phrase like that—"with the so-called peace activist convicted two years ago of destroying federal property at Port Ruh Naval Base. There is evidence he planned much worse, but we cannot divulge details."

"Oh yes, police with their secret evidence." Mom's eyes blinked fast. She sat on one end of the couch, next to her ashtray; smoke puffed between the words. "Governments."

"Beyla, the girls don't need to hear all this." Dad had been getting comfortable in his wing chair, under the enameled wall clock that had once been Granma's, journals stacked up by his feet. "They can draw their own conclusions. Besides, little pitchers tend to spill what they hear."

"Hanna and Mara aren't so little." Then Mom went silent. The news was showing Vietnamese peasant women being marched away somewhere, hands tied behind their backs.

"Should I turn it off?" Dad got to his feet. Squinting,

Mom snatched up her cigarettes. *Don't you girls ever say one word,* Dad had warned once, *when your mother gets like that.*

"Just sit—just sit, Daniel." Mom still seemed calm, but in a moment she would shrink back in the chair, just sobbing, the way she did when she got like that. But never mind—it wasn't Mom's old-Europe memories that were important now, it was what she'd said about secret evidence: the things the FBI told the news could just be lies.

The picture on the screen had been fuzzy, very fuzzy—someone thin and young. He might not be the person out there in the gully.

It was not that she had to listen, over roast chicken dinner at Dad's sister's house, to Mom's complaints and Aunt Ellen's snide remarks while Dad pretended not to laugh and Mom's lips puffed around a cigarette. It was not even that Mom and Dad loved her but they'd never help.

It was the way that, leading Stormy this afternoon from the gully up the red clay path, she'd felt she was walking into an unreal world.

The maroon paint of Aunt Ellen's dining room was like that clay, blood-colored with no way out. Maybe songs could get through what that man was caught in—not only pain or bullets but something else, something he'd done or whatever else made him not try to get well. She should have sung him a different song, the Aaron one. All through Aunt Ellen's *salade niçoise,* she kept thinking about that song.

"Aaron was a scholar but he turned into a hero, he was brave," Granma used to say. Granma's apartment had been full of tiny porcelain figurines and heavy quilts. "The Nazis made us walk through snow until our feet froze," Granma had said once. Aaron had been Granma's son, Mom's big brother. "When the people told the fighters 'Go to the forests,'" Granma would say, "my Aaron said, 'No, we stay here and fight beside you in the ghetto.' Then he told me, 'Ma, you and Beyla have your chance, go take it.' So when the troops came—already it was Passover—your *mamaleh* and I went hiding with Sonja, my Pole. Eight months, until they found us. They sent her to a different camp, so I don't know. But once, years later, a woman came to Washington and told me about my Aaron, how my Aaron died fighting in the ghetto and was brave." Then Granma would sing the fighters' song.

Now, watching Mom and Dad and Aunt Ellen squabble across the dinner table, Mara wondered would Uncle Aaron have been like them, all the arguing.

And none of it was real—not while that person was out there, desperate. Desperate like Granma and Mom had been, and Sonja who had saved them. Desperate as those families—*right this very minute*—being bombed in Vietnam.

Desperate like everyone eventually, because—this was the truest fear—each life had to end.

Aunt Ellen brought the tray of raspberry muffins from the kitchen for dessert, and Mara took one carefully, on its yellow paper napkin. Yes, she should have sung Aaron's song to that man in the gully. Except—sometimes those eyes slitted and looked aside too fast—what if he really was the suspect, the bomber? The bomber had killed people.

Watch out for yourself first. That was what people always said, but this time it was different. Very different. Because now, sitting here next to Hannah at the breakfast table, chewing her toast with cinnamon and reading the newspaper, she *knew*. Knew for sure.

Gavin—that was the name on the news photos, Gavin Hareen. The fugitive, confirmed by the new witness as definitely the man seen skulking, nine days ago, in the brush moments after the explosion. The bomber who had fled, wounded, into the park. They'd catch him soon, the chief was promising; "Call him 'suspect,' if you will, but that's our man." The news showed other photos of him, too—one of a smiling boy around Hannah's age, and one hard to make out but familiar, a man with empty eyes.

Terribly empty. "That park is scary, crazy people out there," Hannah said. But fear was not what was important. What was important was things happened to people; people got shot, got hunted—swatted like bugs. Besides—Mara didn't understand, except it was true—what most frightened her now was the danger to him.

Or maybe this is how a killer strikes; he seems helpless and you start to like him, and then—wham. No, that was being silly; she took another piece of toast.

Rising wind rushed through the woods—thunderstorm approaching. The old square of canvas she had stretched above the man, and camouflaged with leaves and vines, could easily fall, strung between two branches and a narrow root that twisted from the rocky overhang. Now, as she rode around the curve and made out the man's broken form, her fear seemed absurd. He could barely sit up—able to pull himself along the ground but mostly just waiting, patient and still.

A light came into his eyes at her arrival.

Sliding off Stormy, she put down the bag of supplies and, using sticks and a cord, began to shore up the canvas; she pulled more vines across. "Looks like rain," she said. But she kept her distance from where he sat half-slumped against the low clay cliff. Because he did seem stronger.

"What's scaring you?" He blurted the question. "You are scared, now I can move around?" With a little smile, he added, "Well, sort of move."

It was absurd; she wanted to cry. No, to flee—only, she had to show him the news photos. If he really was innocent and the police searched here and found him, he wouldn't even know why. But if he was the bomber, and if he saw she understood just who he was, he might—

No, Sonja didn't flee, back there in Poland.

So she held up the paper she'd found at the Chevy Chase bus stop. His eyes scanned the page—the article on "tiger cages" in Saigon, a feature on Bolivian miners, the headline "Witness Confirms Flag Day Bomber i.d."

None of it seemed to sink in. "They're hunting you," she said. "It says 'Gavin Hareen.' It says you bombed an army truck, and the bomb tore apart two soldiers and some woman—she was just walking by, through the park."

He didn't seem to even see the photos. "*You* think that? Of me?"

"Three people." Her voice went hard—why hadn't he reacted when she'd said people were "torn apart"?—but she heard her own squishy fear, the awareness of staying safely outside his reach. "That's what they say."

He took the paper, started to read, then looked all around, like someone stunned. "No. No, they couldn't think that." He bit his lips, then went so still she wanted to cover her eyes. "Unless—" His fingers pulled at the tiny stones in the cliffside.

Her heart thumped. Whatever it was, she didn't want to know. Because, if he were—no, that made no sense. Could make no sense. "Gavin—"

He laughed—briefly. "That's my name."

"'Unless' what, Gavin?" She shifted her feet. Ready to run. *Far too dangerous, here in the woods.*

He rolled one of the tiny stones, white like a miniature marble, between his fingers. "You know I've done time? Like, stuff against the war."

"'Done time'?" Been in jail, he meant—must mean. And so of course then they'd suspect him. Yes. Maybe that was all it was.

"Here." He'd picked up another stone and held it out— even smaller, white-pink granite. "You want one?"

She shook her head, hoping the tears wouldn't come. "You'd better say." The log she sat on was too close, but she almost didn't care.

The mockingbird was at it again. Two shapes like blue jays swung into the dogwood.

He had glanced toward the jays, toward the cliff.

"Those soldiers." But he kept avoiding answering. Like somebody guilty.

Already, it was nearing sunset. At the stable they'd be getting worried, "Mara's got that horse out late again?" They might come looking; the risk to him was enormous. He seemed only half aware of it. "Don't you believe all that, okay?" He spoke in that used-up voice, like someone drowning.

Someone trying to reach her.

Or trying awful hard to make her believe he told the truth. Getting to her feet, she started to gather up Stormy's reins. Then waited, listening to the blue jays.

Even desperate, Gavin was a gentle person, someone frightened like she was. Again, he held out the tiny stone; it shone white and made her smile. For an instant, he smiled back—so widely she had to look away. Then the little stone touched her palm; very lightly, she stretched her fingers around it. Up in the dogwoods, the mockingbird kept singing.

It wasn't the bombing scared her.

"Mara?"

She barely heard him.

"Mara, you're the kindest person I've ever known." He

was pulling himself to his knees, leaning against a white-bark tree. A smudge of clay coated his right elbow. "I don't want you to keep thinking I . . ." *A caring person.*

"Those kids, see. I could not stop thinking about it—about My Lai, those kids and moms."

If she got home late, she'd be scaring Mom.

Tears had started running down Gavin's cheeks. The cough tore his breath, and he slid to the ground. Even though she knew better, one of her hands reached out; it landed awkwardly on his shoulder. And all at once, before she could pull away, he'd bent over her other hand, and lifted the palm to kiss it.

Mom and Granma were innocent. Sonja who saved them was innocent.

Making herself still look at Gavin, she took two steps back to the horse, lifted up the reins. "I've got to get Stormy to the stable now." She swung into the saddle. "Crying can't bring dead people back."

Only, it wasn't just that, not really. It was that he was no longer the same person. Past the heat-stifled dogwoods, sunset still reflected on the muddy creek, and she would still return to help him, still keep his secret. But nothing was the same, and couldn't be.

Deconstructing Desdemona; or, Escape from the Belly of the Cold War

> *Twas pitiful, 'twas wondrous pitiful.*
> *She wished she had not heard it, yet she wished*
> *That heaven had made her such a man.*
> —*Othello*

All right, Michael, yeah—sure, if only President Kennedy had lived. And agreed, the Tonkin Gulf "attack on our ships" is a red herring, the Cuban blockade didn't turn into Armageddon—but, see, playing "What if the past had been different?" is like trying to resuscitate a corpse. I mean, not just Cuba but, even now, what people say speaks only their *suspicions*: have we really peered *enough* beneath those missiles' surface (as it were)? What was the Soviets' *real* motive?

Oh but wait—dear Michael, I'm so sorry! It's hardly a moment, seated here in the Med over coffee, for political analysis; you have real sorrows—you too, just like me. Let's leave the world's troubles awhile, agreed—better focus on our own. God knows, they're ugly enough, our private things. We've known each other only how long, eh? A year now? Since we met, anyhow—and yes, I keep safe all your stories, my shaggy Michael. Sure—so come, let's relax here, safe, in the stupid noisy café's upstairs corner, not dark-lit but no one'll overhear us through the crowded clatter if we speak privately here, tonight, about what hurts us. Because I understand how much you suffered from it, your dear friend's dying. Barely a month— if even that long?—before we met; I remember your sorrow. And how you thought, even then, you might, in some true sense, perpetuate his life if only you could dare tell his story—that he might thus endure to future generations. Michael, please know I understand.

Yet, tell me this: did you lie on his grave all night, really? And why so many medical details? For, doctors treat the sick as bodies, and if this helps the treatment, good, but whom does verbal treatment save? Isn't such detail redundant as replying history? Or is it something else? Experience is far from words. But does this question seem rude, a challenge, Michael? Please know it challenges also my very right to ask, and thrusts not at motives but at clichés. No? I don't mean do not speak of him, of what occurred, but . . . from your heart, if you can, not twisted under facts' minutiae.

Or—no? Oh very well, then, would you rather we talk of oubliettes, and watch the sunset through the café's windows—anything but speak of how we forget, deny, remember?

Sorry, Michael, forgive my rudeness. Please. Sure, tell me again of that night you lay along your loved friend's grave. Only, this time, of what you felt—how futile his death, how broken—of sorrow and sympathy.

And—all right, Michael, yes; I *will* tell you. I *will*—of once by night, the big red room, and Murph.

And of Mia, too, sitting on the couch, and Robert, rocking in Murph's ornate chair, and I, seated on the rug in Murph's red room, November, '61. Nobody worried yet what Cuba *really hid* beneath its skirts. I'd been speaking, as it happened, of the mind-body problem, of consciousness, awareness of another's mind, philosophy, not of the Cold War's nuclear terror. Spread out before us on Murph's table were New York filet, grilled potatoes, little peas, later chocolate croissants, and Mia said this would cost thirty dollars in San Francisco, across the bridge. And—oh but now I too am doing it, details upon details. Whereas what mattered were the feelings in that room.

Robert rocked and talked, and Murph. I did not look at Robert, though he spoke; I listened, but I looked at Murph. And there—I noticed, in the same vague, slightly angry (or, rather, stressed, intent) way I had, before—there was something strange about Murph's face. Everyone sat—chatting, and he and Robert, for maybe thirty minutes, took turns spinning a silver sheath-knife through the air. Then, after we'd all finished eating and the knife and last croissant been put away, we sat on in the big red room and talked about the tests Robert was giving to his students (to discover, he said—don't laugh, Michael—"creatives"). We played with the tests, Murph picked up one test, and—our discussion having again turned philosophical—"That last question, Rob?" Murph asked, "The one, you know, 'Has your soul ever left your body?'"

Robert looked down, grinned, "Hey, I didn't write that question."

"Good. Since it's absurd. I died—I mean, my heart stopped, from my wounds—but I still wouldn't know how to answer that one." At which point (even though the question was one we all have about death), we—let me tell you—just laughed and laughed, and thought we'd better, *damn right*, go along with Murph's laugh at his words. But we each of us felt it; I felt it in me and from Robert and Mia; it hung there in the room, suspended, shiny, from the ceiling. So, being still capable, then, to handle shocks and other conversation-stoppers—and also still thinking myself clever in philosophy, I said, "So, *did* it?"

And Robert, socially attuned if not especially empathetic, said, "Yes, Murph, don't stop *there*. Tell us what happened."

Then, I, "So where'd it go? Your soul?"

And Murph, "Well, how should I know? I was unconscious."

So we all laughed. Very witty and clever, this—if you happened to be a young student in analytic, Wittgensteinian philosophy (with its own language-game of the quick "criterion," the even faster "verify," standing as entry posts to emerging wit).

But meanwhile, let me ask *you*, Michael: if someone returns from the dead and tells of his experience, would you believe him? And if so, how so?

No—no, I wish I could say this kindly. Michael—what if your friend had come, had appeared, and hugged you, that night, hugged you tightly through your stained old army jacket, there on his chilling grave?

But in the red room that dark November, saying "You couldn't be both dead and unconscious," I slapped my hand, in a clichéd, burlesqued, strangely energetic act, across my forehead, rolled my eyes, and cried "Christ, what a time to be asleep!" And my half-baked would-be flippancy evoked a strange confusion (perhaps my act too forced, too false a fight against something unsettling and too serious, or perhaps the others simply failed to follow the veiled feelings and illogic of my outburst). In any case, there was more false, embarrassed laughter, a near-instant ripple in the smooth of that discussion (yet for an instant only; we were so absorbedly quick-witted a group—dare I say Wittgensteinian?).

Clichéd, you think? Well, meanwhile Murph, or was it Robert, put the knife back on the floor. Everything turns on a Freudian slip, you know. On a word.

Smiling, I held my gaze ahead, pretending to be unperturbed. I realized that my outburst had been less to protect those here who'd been too near to loss or death, than to, like a vast umbrella, shield and protect myself.

I had lived, as a student, too alone in my mind. That month, I found in Murph a closeness of experience and thought, a need for independence, much, I thought, like my own. Our closeness was so new—fresh, believe it!— we would chat and walk together everywhere, Murph and I, always laughing.

Then, just before Christmas, people in the next apartment gave a party, and in those days I often looked beautiful; that night, I did. This was a Friday, and on Monday, the night after Christmas, Murph showed me he wanted me. In his big red room, only the two of us, we drank champagne, and there we were, leaning along the rug and talking, just slouched there on the rug and laughing, and then talking ever more softly, still drinking champagne, and then—

Michael, who the fuck are you? Because you sit there on that scrollwork café chair, watching with that sympathy I don't—

No, look, I shouldn't pretend—of course I've told someone, before. I have—and still I feel guilty. If it is guilt. (Or perhaps it, too, is "enjoyment"? Snicker. "Freeing the unconscious vipyrs," as they say. Or as somebody might say. Maybe.)

—and then I looked at Murph across the ashtray and the cigarettes, our empty glasses and the champagne bottle, on that Monday evening after Christmas; and I wanted him. I saw he'd been wanting me too, and I tried to stretch out my hand gently, tremulously. But I had been drinking, I was awkward. And so my hand fell, neither gently nor exquisitely (although not roughly), simply landed sturdily, on his shoulder.

I mean—Michael, I'd *wanted* this, yet longed for that "first touch"—that first exquisite (what's called "tremulous") touch. (Perhaps a not unfamiliar concept?) A shivering gentleness, I'd wanted, a trembling hesitation. . . .

Well, it didn't work that way. And, shoving aside the ashtray and the cigarettes and glasses and the bottle, taking off his glasses, all in one split-second motion, Murph pulled me tight against his body. Not roughly—but, you see, I had had too many unrequited loves, too many fantasies. There had even been, twice in the past, a first touch after hours of the agony of longing, a touch full exquisite—poignant.

My point is, Michael, when I think that what came later, in January, might not have happened had these Monday-after-Christmas-night moments been different—that I might not in January have reacted as I did had I, this first evening, felt the tremulous, longed-for connection—I mean, if we'd not been drinking champagne and if our first touch had been fragile, even deeper—perhaps what later came and ruined so much wouldn't have happened . . .

Unlike some people, however, I question such hypotheses. I'd had not only first-touch fantasies—of course not. Besides, I *won't* put forth some Freudian theory, some single hypothesis, as "explanation." Consider there've also been, not long ago, the fantasies of the man whom I would save by lifting from him, through feeling it in *my* body, his pain. And you know, I'm not the only woman has such fantasies.

Yes, the way we may believe we've telepathy, not simple empathy, for the wounded, the maimed.

How close you are, my poor friend, in your story, your experience, but you've not always seen. One must fight the given tones, the clichés, that may obscure truths. And the ironies, self-references, and private jokes we raise, as fragile barriers, in guilt. For we feel guilt.

And indeed, among the people on another day in Murph's red room, a shining aura, as if a silver razor blade, hung sharp, suspended. "How deep," somebody—Murph or Robert—said metaphorically, "How deep that cuts." It slashed right in.

Because—Michael, as I told you, I'd vaguely noticed something strange about Murph's face, and had realized those unsettling marks, not beautiful nor ugly but always noticeable, were scars. I had connected all this, of course, with the discussion "Where'd the soul go?" back in November; still, I'd not much more thought about it. But, after Murph pulled me close, that Monday-after-Christmas night, and I put my arms around his shoulders, the scars were there, and I could feel them. And when I touched his chest.

Well, that was all. His face, his chest, his arms. At some moment, you know, I realized—these, the steel that made these, had nearly killed him.

Michael, there is horror in me as I tell you this. But there is something else, something that comes in the mouth and is like wanting to cry. It is like what I felt one summer day when, a little girl, I sat beside my parents and my brother opened the right-hand car door, and someone (there is guilt, and I think *It was I*, though in point of fact it was not I) accidently closed the door upon his thumb. There was shock in me, and a feeling, *before* there could be knowing, before I *could* have sensed what had happened, of wanting this *not to be*, and a clutching in my mouth. I wanted to suck and soothe the thumb, mine or was it his, to make *this not have happened*. To heal the thumb, make this *not* be.

You understand? Yes, of course you do.

Michael, remember, this spring, the earthquake? I'd gone with two other women to spend Good Friday weekend on the beach, and, that night, an earthquake hit Alaska and the tidal wave came down the coast. And, you know, it was as with my brother in the car, that childhood day long before, because I saw, across the sand, a girl come running from the sea and realized she'd almost drowned—and that I'd not seen, not known—that what *had not been known* suddenly was there. With this came guilt; I wanted, *needed*, to have risked to drown with her, to *have been with her* and saved her from the ocean. Yet knew it was too late, what was could not be undone.

Yet, earlier on that beach, I'd ordered a child in from the water, saying "Suppose there's an earthquake?" and stood on the sand and heard the waves. *How the water knifes in, perhaps drowns our time.* Fear the deadly elements, not only death.

Oh, damn, I'm sorry—done too much of the talking tonight. But you know, when you—hardly only you—speak of depths, sometimes your tone implies it is okay, may even communicate feeling, to speak in mere clichés. As if cliché void of true sentiment might nevertheless fuse with insight. Still, I guess that's not absurd—if you ask the right questions. If, that is, you ask the questions and aren't hypnotized by familiar, clichéd rhythms, by words in too evident patterns when one recognizes something seeming like a feeling one's actually known. I mean—Michael, you're a poet—and an elegant and café-haunting poet at that, a veritable queen (if I'm using the term right?) among your friends—thus truly an original wit who would utterly eschew clichés. For poets seek truth, are often philosophers; isn't that what we say? Philosophers eschewing clichés, though perhaps over-steeped in philosophy jokes—that is, in meta-jokes, deep waters beneath the rippling current.

Or rather, that's how we *did* speak—okay, maybe not you, but most those I knew back then. Then, meaning in that big red room, that year, '61, eleven months before the Cuban Crisis. In November and the late-December night of that year. The year when Murph first . . .

Oh, but see? See? I, too, evade.

All right, then, Michael, here it is. I've said I knew Murph had these scars from near-death, and I've spoken of the closeness we'd begun to find together. And, that evening after Christmas, he held me close and, clinging to him, I felt as if my hand would smooth, could make these scars go away, and we . . . No, but I thought this was wrong, that there should be only desire.

Oh wait—dear Michael, dear Michael, would you rather—?

Ah no. Sorry, *I* need speak, yes, not evade; I shall tell you. For I know how you have come to understand this, know how you and your beloved friend both tried so hard. So very hard. I know what you tried to overcome, what scars. And yet—listen to me—do not think you understand too well. Even though you have been there and there is much you know.

But what I want to tell you—please let me—is this: had that first touch been different, had the desire and tenderness that gives the life of touch to bodies been expressed and fought the recognitions that may turn thoughts, bodies, to repeat some frantic moment past—had desire, that December evening, fully bloomed— . . . But this did not happen, and instead, with January, the world turned into . . . what it turned into—call these the cutting elements, knives in deep waters, shaken swallowed tears, "regret."

Murph held me closely, walking through the pretty, holiday-lit streets in drizzly Christmas rain. And that night I dreamed of a scarred old man climbing up the tree and through my window, and the eye that watched behind the pillow. "You *wanted* to kill me," a dream-Murph in the pillow said.

When I'd tried everything, the beach girl's mother said, "Let's not take the children too far out. The ocean's dark water can drown."

No, I can tell you "why"—so many "why"s—yet remember that guilt can double with detail. As you learned with your story—or rather, your *friend's* story. Yet, please know, I see no guilt in you, Michael, and I'm sorry, sad for you that he died. But, like you, I ask do we use these pasts, pasts not our own, as if to save ourselves—much as we'd save those we speak of—through a public immortality. Isn't this *your* "strange thought," too? For *of course* there may be guilt, *of course* it may also be ourselves we'd save. That's not strange, simply a cliché, to want immortality and to spread what we've known to our world. Surely for this there is forgiveness. Oh—sorry for these religiously loaded words. But, listen, can the fantasies be absolved— like mine, the one I told you, of taking the pain from a loved person who otherwise might have died? But what if we would turn our "beloveds" into, basically, no more than their stories? While *we* go forth to tell those stories (but clichéd, so the world may think it understands).

No. No—b.s. Listen, Michael, clearly I'm being slippery here, dancing the over-*literati* dark fandango of the symbols in the sky—or, like, y'know, peeking beneath that skirt in Cuba for some alien *spies*! Guess why. (Hint: self-referencing evades. And—oh hell—the philosophy student still, at moments, climbs a metaphorical dais and would speak.)

But—let's get serious—have you ever asked a person for their story? Because a story can come forth too soon, like a first touch—told before you care enough, or awkwardly—or when you've begun to care too much. Yet, rightly timed, a story draws us (is this empathy? Or love or need?) and holds us in its time, cuts into us with poignancy (or is this idea only a story-teller's *claim*?) Yet whatever else, surely—don't we know by now?—a form of empathy, a giving and gift. Remember, there are tales and fantasies of darkness, and of hope.

Michael, never mind. Look, if I now question these Kennedy memorials, those tearful stories of "our" Green Berets carrying women from "guerrilla dens" in Viet Nam—and, yes, the details of why your beloved friend shot himself—please know I question also my own choice of tales to tell. Of course. Back in '61, that Christmas night, I had not questioned enough, though. Or on any night before, or on that New Year's, either.

Realize, I had heard so many stories—laughing where requisite, speaking the proper words in proper tones, content to be told of depths yet feeling none deeply. I'd even told Murph of my "listening style," and there too we were close, both listeners who knew the trade. (For *trade* it is, like right now, seated here by the Med café railing—'cause, wow, I owe you for listening, tonight's airing so one-sided though that was never my conscious intent.)

Okay? So. All right. Back, then, to that New Year's night. When again we sat in the big red room, Murph and our usual group—I this time mostly quiet, I who've no knowledge of real war—and Robert's friend, the guy who'd been in "Special Forces," speaking, "So, like, I walked into that tent there but, oh man, I'd joined up thinking to help those gooks, not to. . . . See, this one guy, they knew he was a Viet Cong—a commie, as we'd say—they'd done both his ears already, and Jack looked over at me and said, 'Man, come on in, come help us with the slicing.' To make Charlie talk. Except he wouldn't talk. I had to"—Robert's friend grimaced—"to ditch my good gloves, 'counta the blood would stick to them. Back state-side, soon I started having guilt." Robert patted his friend's hand briefly, said he hoped psychotherapy could help him.

I slipped from Murph's arms and went into the bathroom and started to vomit; then Murph came in. "This is why you worry me," he said, "I mean, worry for *you*." But that wasn't what he meant.

Yes, this was New Year's night, and cold out, and the room felt, the whole time Robert's friend kept speaking about "Charlie" (or, at times, "damn Viet Cong"), exactly the way it had felt back in November, Mia and Robert again laughing, and I—once past the nausea—trying to join in; and among our wine glasses there hung, suspended in a shining aura, a razor blade to slash into our words and minds. So, still socially adept (and not yet so self-conscious), "You *had guilt*," I said. "What a strange phrase!" Murph listened, unperturbed. (Was I expecting support?)

Michael, last year when we sat here—on these little metal chairs, overlooking an utterly identical coffee line—and I first tried to tell you of these things, I'd already begun thinking maybe they arose in me (and you, and in all of us) from social currents swirling through us, constant or toward some yet unseen crescendo. Zipping along—one might say, as if philosophically—like Leibniz's monads spinning out our selves and futures. But I eschewed these easy, not to mention over-intellectualized, "explanations." For, when we see our thoughts as merely "symbolic of the world," we must wonder, *Am I not guiltier to turn my guilt to symbol and, for instance, tell another's story*? It's action changes lives—action, not story. Besides, you're right—I get too trapped in mind, in dumb clichés, in fearful habitudes; I should come out, march with you people, trust more. March for the world, and trust, and stop evading—oh yes, how often I "evade."

You know, I've called so many things "evasion."

And so—yes, yes, I really will say, now. Yes—yes, Michael. Now.

All right.

It was after I'd stopped puking, and I'd brushed my teeth, and Robert's friend was gone; New Year's was over. It was '62 now, people already asleep here and in Cuba, and, in the red room, Robert and Mia had finally gone. I started taking down the mistletoe, reaching for it in the doorways where it hung. I said, "But, you know, Murph, I can't always trust you." Because, see, I *had* to understand.

Murph stretched out on the couch; he reached with one arm and pulled me down beside him. "You will. I've told you, I won't hurt you."

And—though every censor in me cried *No!*—"But you're so evasive, Murph," I said. "All this stuff about how I 'shouldn't bother with' mistletoe, and never a word about whether you really. . . ." No, I dared not finish the phrase. Because suppose, after all, for him ours wasn't a deepest love but merely a fling. "About whether you— how you," I said instead, "how you got hurt, how you got those scars—what happened."

Michael, I still can't accept the guilt—or is it: can't stop feeling guilty? Yet by now, you'd think, one would . . . should . . .

No. Never mind—*not* to evade more. Here. Here is what I said—"When I asked, you never really answered."

"There were four," Murph said; he wasn't evading. "Four guys. Armed. They sliced very deep. Very—down to the bone." And a few other details. "I tried to get between," he finished, "to save the kid. He died, though." *And I*, he didn't have to say, *lived.*

106

All through the long New Year's night, I stroked him—around his beautiful eyes, and he smiled at me, understanding, loving. I traced that scar along his cheek, and he smiled like a cat. And he gently laughed. (Suppose he cared, you see, enough to laugh?) Michael, he told me there was, sometimes when he held me, violet in my eyes.

Remembering those hours now, the time before the guilt came down, it's like a crumbling wall where long, sweet grass once bloomed.

AND, MICHAEL, THERE IS VIOLET IN MY EYES.

(Oh, sorry. Sorry, please excuse my shout. But, Michael, dear friend, how easily such words as his . . . how easily they pulled me in. I think he cared, you see. Cared truly.)

We had another week. Then one morning, someone on Telegraph Avenue was arguing our forces should "stop coddling peasants" and, that afternoon, while reading in *Time* about bomb shelters "in case the commies are secretly building up—" I felt my old, recurrent *fear of death*. Yes, yes, all that despair stuff, the "I who now am, I who—I, in three years, in eighty, in—*I* will not *be*"—yeah, that despair stuff we all know, clichéd. Yet life, like war, can't be dismissed as "Oh, clichéd!"

So then I felt . . . what's my point, you ask.

Okay.

Okay. So, all right. All right, Michael. Now no more evading.

And after I'd cooked the groceries and we'd eaten and

I'd washed the dishes, in Murph's red room as the evening darkened (a bit later now, already a week into January), I brought up exactly that "fear of death" (pretending this topic did not make the razor hang closer, aura glistening); Murph poured our drinks; he lit our cigarettes. Then we seemed to talk of wars and crises and what lies beneath them, though the razor hung above us, and then to songs that folks in such times sing. To songs, that is, and stories—stories, and the enjoyment of stories. (And note here, Michael, I had not asked, did not ask, what I longed to—about him, me, us.)

"Like you enjoyed the story of my wounding."

"No," I said—but blushed. (I've told you that I blush.)

"Oh yes." Murph sat up on the couch. "You enjoyed it." He leaned far forward. His eyes looked down at me; I couldn't look away. Because—

No, no, I am avoiding—you see, again I've evaded. Even with you. Murph had said much more than this. Had told me, in that long New Year's night the week before, details—many details. "They sliced, you know," he'd said. "They kept slicing. Sparing the arteries, to make it last. The big one did my brother first, and while the kid cried, Jeffrey—the heavy one—and Rod pushed me over the ledge. And jumped down and—"

Collapsing huddled at his feet, I'd said, "No, no, don't," to try to make him stop. To make it stop. Make what had happened have stopped. "Don't, don't say more. I can't—" My lips against the blankets at his feet.

"All right," he'd said, with no expression. "I won't."

But on this evening the next week, when he said, "Yeah, you enjoyed the story of my wounding," and I blushed and couldn't look away, he told me what the doctors had had to do—told me in detail. I huddled again in the blankets, hiding my face away. By 8 o'clock, it was over.

All over. On the radio, a soldier on the news recounted a jungle skirmish, "We can never be sure, out there, what Charlie's up to," adding "They're sharp as knives." And I blushed.

A half hour later, "Sharpest blade you'll ever find," a television commercial began, and I blushed. And after that. . . .

Because, dear Michael, everything relates to what one would forget, once one's aware.

Spring would come, two months later, with poison oak—and a constant itch worse than what even that plant's sap can normally raise. Along with dreams of strange growths on my legs—black, bleeding; I'd hack them off with a silver razor, but they would grow back. We would stay inside, those months; outside, someone might say . . . *words*, and I would blush. There would be topics we'd avoid—I might blush.

And of course you know what a blush *is*? It is a visible acknowledgment of what we dare not face. Which of course is trivial, mere metaphor—except, the poison oak was on my arms, my cheeks, quite as if a gang had lurked outside and bloodied me.

We didn't go out. You understand. Too well, I'd think.

Yet, since then—since a year after Murph left, worn down by my withdrawals, my evasions—there have been the fantasies, often, of saving, of feeling the Other's pain and lifting it away from him, taking it into myself to heal—to heal him—only him? Through my soul.

Michael, thank you! I didn't know the Med carried chocolate croissants—how kind of you, going again through the coffee line to bring them for me.

Ah, and you wanted to check out that third guy in line, the one in the blue shirt? But he couldn't be much over sixteen, you know.

No, no, you're right; better to look instead at the ritual of "questioning motivations." All such hypotheses, too many issues—or ideations?—of "identity," hang heavy on us all, dear friend.

And, please, help yourself, it's a fine croissant. And, please, let's skip into words like "verity," "criterion," all that, and simply say that things like—for me, then— blushing, poison oak, all these *behaved like* symbols. And, in my case, the real issue was that these very symbols could *unmask* me. The danger, I thought—as even the youngest, most backward recruit on an army's jungle trek soon learns—lay in *what lies beneath the surface.* For, after all, we had learned "*Your* mind is not *this other person's*" (a logical necessity), "and therefore to understand, to enjoy—let alone, to empathize with—another's feeling must be *strange, cannot* be your *real* motivation; rather, your true response must lie far *underneath*—must be *ex-*

plained."

As if, beneath those Cuban skirts too visibly near our waters, strange enjoyments lurk to drag us into dubious currents. "You will be guilty, if you blush."

"If, that is"—enjoined on each of us, in our own ways—"your feelings show."

As if, Michael, walking toward that boy in line, you had too widely smiled, then feared to ever smile again.

I know, I know, dear Michael. Your poor beloved friend, to have so despised himself.

But it was still many weeks before the poison oak, still January, a week or so after New Year's, when Murph said "You enjoyed it." First on that New Year's night, and again a week later while I blushed, shamed, saying "Murph, don't," for he'd told me yet more.

But, Michael, why do *I* tell you?

He'd said, "Twelve years—twelve years ago, now. I tried to keep fighting—save the kid, if possible. Not from loyalty; I loved him."

Michael, help. How frightening love can be.

"Until they banged his head so it broke. Then, while Jeff and Alex held me, Jeff turned his knife to make me—" There were ways they'd cut, he'd said. "A dark alley, you know? Like in a movie. Cold, in August? But it chilled my soul. I couldn't live *or* die, in those hours."

Oh, but whose clichés, these? But then, at last truly *hearing*, I fell forward—even as I tell you this, Michael, I shake my head, my lips drawn back in horror—fell across him, lips against his neck and cheek, and—this I tell you—my lips moved on his neck like wanting to cry, while something hung close like knives (not *poignant*, no, a *horror*) as I said, "But, Murph, you are alive."

Well, again, *clichés*.

Heavy, Michael!
"Under the spreading chestnut tree,
I sold you, and you told me!"
    Le veau d'or est vainquer des dieux!
    Dans sa gloire derisoire,
    Dans sa gloire derisoire—
Not everyone thinks so, Michael.
    For thine is
    Life is
A million uses for clichés, you see? The point is, do they at times speak truthfully?

Michael, how good to see you again! Should've known you'd be here at the Med. So, you've published your Baldwin review? Man, that is great.

Me? Nothing much. But lately I've been thinking of catharsis—pity and fear. Of the meanings in tragedies. Thinking, most recently, that perhaps beneath responses we may sometimes take as dire, our world's reflected in our feelings' depths, clear and beautiful so we reach out again to give to what we've felt (yes, often outside us)— and see reflected there.

And you, too, haven't you felt this new hope in the

world, Michael, heard the people lately speaking, watched friends go South working for justice, seen—

No—no, *wait*! Michael, what are you *saying*? That *can't* be. In Birmingham? The Baptist church where demonstrators gather? Four little girls, bombed to death. While we were sleeping.

I'd just got home from the Vietnam Day rally when there was an earthquake and I ran outside. A woman was standing on the sidewalk with her little boy. Still shaky, we shared a cigarette. She said she grew up in Cuba; no one had wanted the missiles there. She'd been newly married; "We had such plans!" Once her husband gets his degree, they and their boy will move to Chile, "but someday we go home, to live our lives in Cuba. It's what we've always wanted."

A quarter million people marched in New York City today against the war, and a hundred thousand here. "November, '69, way *way* past time to bring the boys back," one speaker said, "and, for God's sake, time—Nixon or not—to stop suspecting Commies under every bed."

To stop suspecting the Other, the self.

Believe me, I too wish your friend had lived to see Stonewall—seen men dare struggle for their right to openly love men. Well, of course, just as we've all learned *every* love is beautiful. You know, *now* it sounds clichéd— "You too are beautiful," "Stop wars—give life," "We each can love. Each needs someone to love." Yet true.

Dear Michael, my feet still hurt so from the march, and tonight's another planning session, I'd like so much to kick back with you here on the Med's little balcony and watch the people dancing on the Avenue. But of course we have to stop the War, gotta keep on keepin' on, *la lutte continue*, yes? For, otherwise . . . how many more loves and years will be lost before enough people recognize that the frightening, enticing depth we've each felt was—is—simply love and empathy? Reminding us we do care—"we," who, even when frightened or unsure, long to act—will act—caring, to save loves and lives.

Chasing Leads

To risk herself, fully and lovingly, against the war—to save the struggling people of Vietnam. Those were what mattered. Not whether Ricardo ever loved her—not whether her fear had pushed him away. The single thing that really mattered now was to find the caring people, to become like them—and, at their side, create a world where no one would be killed, no one be bombed, where war would not be possible.

Lifting her cigarettes from the kitchen table, Nora forced calm upon her thoughts still jangling in the amped-up "Monday, Monday" from the radio out in the Berkeley Barb's front office.

Simply find the caring people; simply stop the massacre in Vietnam.

"You're not working?" Max, the *Barb* editor, bearded and grungy in jeans and a denim jacket, leaned in the doorway, dangling his empty coffee cup. "Better get a move on, Nora. And a new pot brewing. Don't you know it's copy *and* coffee makes this paper run? Except, it's a mess this week—all you Lefties wait 'til it's practically deadline."

Which was true enough, deadline was at midnight tonight, not even an hour away, yet no word from the union on hospital negotiations, nothing from the YSA about the rent strike, no date even set for the Peace Jam.

"Jeff and Barry want coffees, too."

"Okay, okay, Max." Grabbing a can of Folger's, she stepped across to the stove. Two weeks ago, the hip attorney she'd been interviewing on the U.C. campus had glanced up, saying, "All I can tell you is some *very dedicated persons* plan to shut it down." Meaning the UTC napalm plant in Redwood City. "Nonviolently, yeah, but they're planning lots more than civil disobedience." So those very dedicated persons might be ones who cared and would risk everything. But no way to know for sure—and, after days of trying "likely" phone numbers, she still hadn't found them. Still, if they were the people who cared enough . . .

Jeff was finishing up in the photo-processing closet; Barry, skipping coffee, had headed out the door; and finally she gave up on the Redwood City group. If it even existed. She tossed her hair and flipped open her steno pad. *Forget that stuff. Just get the VDC story so you can head home.* Though "story" was too strong a word. With LBJ prepping to bomb Hanoi and Haiphong, and China poised to act if the war enlarged, the VDC—Vietnam Day Committee, last year's spearhead of antiwar struggle—was calling a "Movement Picnic." *Right. Make it a short-short, hey. Recipes and all.* Lifting the phone receiver, she dialed the VDC.

But no one answered. "Guess they're not on night watch, Max."

From his desk, the editor tossed a yellow card through the kitchen doorway; she caught it between two fingers.

"That number'll work," Max said. "Dave used to be on Steering Committee. And don't worry, he's up—it's dark outside."

On the eighth ring, a man's voice answered, half asleep. It turned sharp at her question. "Fuck, babe, how do I know? See, I know *nothing* about that picnic. That's how we're gonna end the war, right? A picnic? You want a story, how come you're not covering Redwood City? People down there are—"

"You know about Redwood City?"

"Oh." The voice went quiet. "Yeah. Yeah, I do. Sure, I've a whole portfolio of stuff. Pictures, photos of napalm bombs, everything. You know what those napalm trucks look like? Those silvery crates full of shiny bombs?"

She hesitated, not sure why. "You've got photos?"

"If you're serious, yeah. Give me an hour, I'll drive over there."

"We're on deadline." She stared into the phone, not

sure what made her say it. "Get here in fifteen minutes. *If you really want to end the war.*"

An hour later, he slid into the *Barb* office and, noiselessly crossing the kitchen, dumped his portfolio on the kitchen table, covering the papers she'd been studying.

"Take some coffee." She nodded toward the pot.

"Yeah. That's what I should drink. Coffee." Lean-faced, with blond hair cut too short, he was watching her reaction out of hard, ice-blue eyes. His lips curved down in a cheerless grin.

Then she realized who this was—"VDC Dave," the "adventurist" said to have emptied the Berkeley draft board office with a cardboard "pipebomb," and run a sailboat up to Alameda Naval Air and got the sailors loading ammunition until he'd laughed and they'd had to pull the boxes back off. Above those elegant cheekbones, his eyes kept measuring her. In the steam-filled kitchen, she snapped open the portfolio and tried to focus on reporting.

Because what "VDC Dave" was saying about Redwood City was, after all, unfocused, garbled, yet the way he moved pulled at her body like a noose, and those eyes, still fixed on her like a cougar's on its prey, occluded the space where Ricardo's deep eyes for months had gleamed, even after he'd left her and gone "back home to help my people." Yet she had to piece together something—coherent, hopeful, a call to action—from Dave's press clips and releases. A public meeting in San Jose where women had chained themselves to a napalm factory, photos from a citizens' rally in Redwood City, pamphlets about napalm, a flyer on the upcoming action: "Persons whose consciences impel them will walk onto UTC's death plant and make a silent stand against the war . . ."

"'A silent stand'?" She asked it aloud. "No, but I thought that this time—" *That finally there'd be people risking everything against the war.* The people who love enough, care enough.

"Think again." He was grinning at her, challenging.

No, this man was an adventurist, that cold intensity a clear exaggeration. *And damn well may be an agent—that haircut, tough-talk. Could be the CIA.* She lit a cigarette— her turn now to measure him.

His portfolio, however, held reportorial treasure. Photos of napalm bombs stacked up in pistachio orchards, loose bombs lying along the docks in the Mexican American town of Alviso. "And in San Jose," he added, leaning close behind her and clutching her hand to light his cigarette from hers, "they've bombs stored right beside the road. Unfenced." Reaching into his scuffed backpack, he pulled out a glass jar containing a light, clear jelly. "Guess what?"

She dared not flinch.

"Oh yeah?" He slouched, bracing his back against the wall. "Babe, if *that* scares you, what're you gonna do when we have to fight? Do you know how much of this we're dropping on those people this year? This *week*? Do you really care?"

His judging was relentless. Infuriating. So why did she

forgot everything except his presence barely inches from her, those long-fingered hands she could easily reach.

"Thing is, you have to go now." She spoke crisply, reddening. "Sorry, but I can't write this up while making conversation."

He went silent. Then, "Okay then, come with me, babe, to San Jose on Saturday. We can take a look around at the bombs." Blue eyes fixed on her. "You're not scared?"

She dared not flinch.

Across the rushing Saturday traffic, Nora watched the tract homes flashing by beside the freeway, reminded herself she could change, become more giving and less afraid—and that they could make the nation, too, change, and end its war. She stared hard out the window, away from Dave. She dared not withdraw.

"Look here." Dave was gesturing toward a little valley between the bare hills. She turned her head a few inches, forcing the motion.

"How the hell—?" Letting go the wheel , he squeezed her wrist. "How the fuck will you do anything, when we have to fight, with those nerves?" But at least he was looking at the road again. "See, that's the trouble with the Movement. We're all fucked up."

She closed her eyes. This drive had gone on a full hour now. "It's not us, Dave, it's the System within us that's fucked up." *Closing us down, keeping us from generous love.*

"Yeah, it's us. *Us.*" He smiled, an American movie little-boy smile. How practiced, that guilelessness. Yet her abdomen quivered with desire.

"All the same, Nora, we can act." Again that smile-grin. "Remember last year when the draft board downtown had to close for a month? 'Come back another time, boys, we can't stick around to enlist you'? See, we didn't get those workers out by moral witness. But when those clean, nice citizens sending kids to Vietnam opened those envelopes and saw that elegant 'Warning,' on linen stationery in book bodoni typeface, and read what just might happen, they started thinking fast, 'Suppose the next ones blown away are us?'"

"Yes." Something was turning her voice weak, like a fearful but admiring child's. "Yes, a—a good action, Dave." *If I had your daring . . .*

The van swerved as he glanced at her again. "Don't you understand? Don't any of you understand? We really napalmed that mother and her child. Listen, if people want to demonstrate, if Women for Peace wants to boycott Dow, if the whole damn city sits on its ass expounding 'progressive' slogans—okay, I'll share with them what information I've got, just like with you. But that's it. We've got to do more, babe."

Flowers—lupine, golden poppies, tall white daisies—grew by the roadside, and near the turnoff to Alviso a mockingbird sang on a barbed-wire fence. Beyond a sparse woods glinted a narrow strip of dark water, the southern tip of the bay. Dave pulled the van into an overgrown graveled lane leading to a stonework bridge.

"There's Alviso. And we're out of gas."

He dragged out a gas can from the van's storage section as she looked on, and climbed down. While he stood filling the tank, she stepped from the van and crossed the lane to pick the nearest wildflowers—mostly, blue lupine—amid the warm grass. The bridge formed a high arch over a bubbling creek, birds sang in the oaks, and downslope rose an old wooden church with a tall white steeple, stuccoed houses clustered around it.

"Isn't it strange to find lupine here," Dave called, in a softened voice. "And it's not yet summer." He seemed so gangly, boyish, his eyes hooded. But those eyes demanded, and those deft hands, those sharp cheekbones, drew like magnets.

Caution. Danger. Don't let yourself get used. Were these only old fears?

Dave tilted his head, grinning the movie grin. She stared back, tossed the wildflowers to the ground. They climbed back into the van.

And she realized it hadn't disturbed him: her childish gesture of flinging away the flowers hadn't bothered him. Her heart jumped in glad surprise. No, it hadn't disturbed him at all, as it would have Ricardo or so many other guys she'd known. Suddenly she laughed.

And saw, there ahead of them, a crowd dressed in weekend elegance, probably Alviso residents, who promenaded along the town's long embankment, a levee to hold back the sparkling Bay. Beyond it, across the Bay's narrow estuary, hundreds of shining napalm bombs in open crates gleamed in the bright sun.

Stacked fifteen feet high, the slatted crates of napalm bombs in San Jose rested unfenced beside the highway. David parked the van a half-mile away, outside the city health office, and she followed him back, along the highway's broken curbing, past a shopping center and a closed garage, to a potholed drive. Turning there, they followed the cracked asphalt drive as it curved around until it opened on a sort of roofless chamber. Within, hundreds of bomb-filled crates formed walls, crisscrossed by narrow aisles of more stacked crates that stretched high above their heads. No one could see in here from the highway, or even from the asphalt drive, but her heart pounded, panicky; she couldn't escape.

"Come, come look." Excitedly, crouched over like a cat, David glided toward the farthest corner. She could barely make out his hands in the shadows, see them slide across a crate on the bottom row. Forcing herself forward, she spied the nosecone, sharp inside its housing, already uncoupled from its silvery shell, its long green-and-red cut wires sticking up like antennae of a metal insect.

"Want to borrow my knife, babe?"

She ran her fingernails along the insulated wires, but here—standing sweaty beside this man only yards from the San Jose highway—how these things connected, what they *did*, seemed not quite real. Here, reality was merely pretty, shiny things in boxes.

"A knife's a weapon—that it, babe? You won't even

touch one? What do you think those bombs are for?"

No, what was most real was his pressure. Unending pressure. *Dave, stop, stop telling me what to do.* She knelt beside the first crate, watching him stalk among the rows, crouch here and there above a crate, knife in hand, softly whistling.

Dave, hush. A security guard could come at any moment. Her stomach hurt and, if Dave hadn't brought her, she'd be home safe. This was crazy—time to leave.

"Nora, I realize what you do—making people aware of the news and all—that's important too." Approaching, slippng his knife between the slats of one chest-high crate, he started removing stickers. Four yellow, two purple. She leaned forward to watch.

"You hear me, babe? I know this is a big jump for you."

"True." His words had released her. Quickly, her own hands were reaching out. A moment later, she watched her fingers peel the first sticky papers from the next crate, going faster. Removing those wires might save lives.

"Flammable," the stickers read, "U.S. Armaments— FirebombBLU." For an article, a picture, a possible injunction. She no longer felt sick. From her patchwork purse, she pulled out the Barb's ancient camera and, hands nearly steady, snapped four photos. Caption them well—"Napalm-B—half polystyrene, one-fourth benzine, one-fourth gasoline—superstick stuff that water cannot quench." Write it forcefully, protect people in Vietnam.

"Want my knife, babe? Second chance."

He was right—cutting those wires might save lives. But, now, so could her writing.

To her left, she saw him pull out his cigarettes, shake one from the pack, and hold a lit match toward it. Directly beneath the closest bomb.

Slowly, her gaze met his, and she grinned back—a cat's snarl: *Guess what, Dave, your daredevil stunt's not working on me anymore.*

The flame burned out between his fingers while they stood together against the crates, and she watched his grinning, high-boned face. She wasn't about to stop him, no—wouldn't give him that satisfaction. The flashpoint of napalm was far too high for a match to set off.

Knowingly, she kept on grinning back.

"In my country, they are cruel," Ricardo had said, "but also they are kind"; even leaving her, his hands had trembled in respect, his eyes had gleamed concern. She and Dave lifted two nosecones from the crates and, swinging them with mutual nonchalance, passed between the bomb stacks and started up the driveway to the sunbaked freeway. Risk-taking, yes—clearly he'd risk anything against the war.

Now he turned to her, lifted her free hand in his, "Tiring, babe?" Ricardo's lost deep eyes eclipsed the glacial blue ones; she still had far to seek for those people whose open, generous ways she yet must learn—perhaps among the vigilers outside the Concord Naval Weapons Base, or somewhere else within the blossoming Movement.

But not quite yet. She smiled back, her fingertips' pressure responding to Dave's, and lowered her lashes just a bit.

Ri and Maia

November—Millie

"It was told me here, in this dark-lit kitchen," Millie added, "in those Berkeley years we called the Movement, by the gold light of this lamp." We could still hear the crickets outside in her garden; we'd come inside with her because she'd gone so pale after Ann had asked "But what did happen with that older fellow, Mil—the one from Severino you were so in love with? The guy with the 'I'm just a used-up, broken shell' line? It was a line, you know."

"Wrong, Annie. Wrong," she'd managed. Grabbing a bunch of Kleenex from the sandalwood box on her table, Millie had wiped her eyes, squared her narrow shoulders, tossed her thinning hair. "No line. 'Cause it had really happened. For him, and for that girl. Neither of them older than fifteen, sixteen, back then."

Ri

Yesterday the guys from LaMar School jumped me, downhill where the bus into the city stops. Aurie and that guy Steffan were with them. When I got home, my mother said, "What did they do," my father snapped "Stick up for yourself!" but my brother asked, "What did you do?" What I'd done, in fact, was correct Steffan's answers during class, so he'd look stupid.

Not great of me, or kind to Steffan. But now I know—Aurie's no friend. I'm not hanging out with him tonight—or with his silly sister, either. A major hypocrite, that girl, half the time acting serious about life, and, the other half, off somewhere putting on make-up. They're out there now, her and Aurie both, playing on their lawn like little kids. I can't risk spilling my feather collection, climbing down the vines, but I promised to show it to them. Careful—feathers across the leaves, and everyone'll find out the secret route.

Maia

My name is Maia—Maia Leticia Angelica. I was born on the first day of spring. My people are of good family and courageous; I shall be, too. I want to know Truth, and I think people should walk in the ways of Goodness. All this, I told Ri yesterday. I was practicing my singing when he came in. We talked for two hours. I like Ri. He's smart and no baby, whatever Aurie thinks. He can talk about things. My friend Ana only talks about boys; I've told her so.

Not only that. I told Aurie I know he's one of the kids who ambushed Ri. I said they'd better not. He said, "Says who?" So I threatened to quit playing with him and I told him what I'd tell Daddy unless he behaves.

Ri

While we were exploring, Maia got behind. My brother had already jumped Gold Creek, and so had Aurie; they were laughing at her from the other side. So I jumped, too, and laughed, to show off. Stupid of me—still, she acts like a boy, she wants to come with us, and then she won't jump. But she looked so upset, I said, "You're turning into a young lady, Maia," and teased her until she smiled. Then she jumped the creek with ease, and we caught up with the others and had a good walk to the rapids by Haunted Boulder.

Aurie kept trying to be friendly, but I ignored him— except to ask how his friends that I hit were doing. Later, Maia and I talked about life. She said my father is "a tyrant, and I thought you stood up against tyrants. *I* do." I promised to think about this, since she usually tells the truth. It is rare that people seek truth; my new theory is this is because they fear the truth of death. Which is wise except, hiding from death, they hide from life. Probably they would, anyway.

Maia

We had an important day, on the radio. Then an Army group marched by up the street. They were marching political prisoners to prison at the Base. Ri ran out and threw something at a captain on horseback. I sneaked down to the basement and opened the servants' door so he could escape back inside. But the captain just gave him a lecture. After they left, Ri would not talk to me or anyone until dinner (we invited him to eat with us). During dinner, my mother suddenly said someone left the servants' door open, and I blushed. Then Ri knew what I'd done, and we started laughing. Aurie got indignant. He wants to know the secret, but we won't tell him.

My mother asked Ri if he plans to go to the university someday. It was like she does about my music. Ri finally said, "Oh, I'm volunteering for the Army." My mother had a fit. I laughed, but Ri wouldn't, so I threw a chicken bone in his plate. This resulted in a lecture, later, on lady-like behavior around Young Men of Good Family. I said Ri is just a friend. Then—this is Important—she asked me if I want to go to the conservatory someday, if my singing is good enough.

Ri and I had a serious discussion, too. We talked about how we know Good and Evil. He said I may be right about his father. He said my mother's nosy but nice. I told him I already knew that. I think he has not talked with people about impportant things. Aurie thinks so, too. When we went upstairs, I told Aurie what Ri said about the soldiers, and Aurie said, "That jerk said that?" I got angry

130

and gave him a punch. We started wrestling, and later I was having the Good Feeling and wanted him to return. Only, that's when Mother came upstairs to lecture me.

Ri

I must recognize that Maia is changing, and that I like the ways she's grown. Yet even new maturity is only for a time, and someday the body dies.

We went walking, she and I and Aurie, by the rapids again, searching for snakes and talking about school and aging. It was cloudy and about to rain. The leaves were rotting on the trail, but I saw one still yellow and picked it up. Maia stopped to watch me, so, to tease her, I stuck the yellow leaf in her hair, above her ear. Then my hand tingled. It was electric, like the sky. It made her eyes tear. I climbed down the creek bank after Aurie, in a hurry, and we turned over rocks until we found, curled up under a granite slab, a green snake. We dragged it out and dangled it before Maia's face. She only pretended to be scared.

She was giggling. Then Aurie started making faces and chasing her around a tree, and, while he was doing that, I let the snake go. It is wrong to destroy a life.

But then—to get their attention, since they kept giggling—I started questioning that truth, too. I scared us all; I said, "Do you think the truth of morality depends on the existence of God?" I said, "If not, why couldn't God be evil? And if it does, suppose there isn't a God?" I said we had to risk asking such questions, but they would not answer.

Maia

School bores me. I told Ri I want someday to go ten thousand miles from here and become a concert singer, even if I am a girl. Only, Ri bores me too. He finally got brave enough to ask me to his school party. My mother let me go, after her usual warnings. But when we got there, we couldn't talk, and Ri acted silly like the other boys. I told him I would too dance with another boy if he kept on, so he stomped outside. I could see him through the window, leaning against the fence, thinking.

He kept sulking, even after I apologized, on the Underground coming home. Boys are stupid.

Ri

Yesterday Serenidad had a record snowstorm, and toward evening Maia and I walked through the drifts. We walked in our boots down the streets, hearing nothing but the squish of the snow. Then, past the last estates, we went on to where there's a bare slope down between the fields to the Army Base. We stood and watched; there were two sentries walking around. Maia said one of her parents' cousins was arrested last week, and I asked "Does that scare you?" and she shook her head and laughed. It was the hard, "mature" laugh, but I still felt sorry and wanted to touch her face. I raised my hand, but only to my shoulder.

Then I saw a sled. It was down the road, under a tree.

Maybe some young kids had left it, and I pointed out to Maia its ruts down the slope, already filling with snow. She laughed again, but she shook her head, over and over, when I said "Let's go sledding." She looked so pretty, and she was being so stubborn, that I jumped onto the sled and called, "Maia, come on, climb on."

So she came over and stood there above me. "How?" she said, "Where can I sit?" and I started laughing and got snowflakes in my mouth. "Just climb on my back," I said, and she did, and I kicked the sled off so we went roaring down that hill.

Except, it's not like in a movie; you're trying to steer, and the sled goes really fast. Then I thought, "What if they see us coming, over at the Base, and start to shoot?" I didn't have a gun, and if they did, . . . well, that would be the end for me, yet, dying, still I'd fling my body over to protect her, Maia would be safe.

They didn't shoot, of course. What finally stopped us was a pile of rocks near the bottom. We went bouncing over them—*really* bounced. I lost control of the steering, I could feel Maia start to slip, and I flung out one hand and leg to stop us. Then all at once I slid, and the sled tipped over. Something struck my knee.

It didn't hurt much, it was a rock not yet covered by snow, and the cut's healing already, but for a minute we watched the blood coming out on my leg. I said, "Are you all right?" since she looked so pale and upset. I said, "Are *you* all right?" and she leaned over and took off her gloves and said, "We'd better find something for a bandage."

And then she moved her lips like she was crying, and I felt something new. It was in my skin, in every particle of my skin; it was beautiful. It was in the snow around us—and in us. This time, I lifted my hand and I touched her, her lips, and there was tingling in her lips and in my hand, and in the snow falling between us.

We didn't speak. We held hands coming back, and we walked in our tracks in the snow. It's been thirty hours now and I still can't study. I've read about things like this. But I don't know if this is *real*—can't, until I know what Maia really thinks of me.

Last night, I dreamed we found a forest of purple dragonflies. We held hands, and people wanted to watch us, but they couldn't, and their heads drooped in a great unhappiness, but we knew we were saved and were so grateful to each other; we needed no one else.

Maia

I wish it was Ri who was my brother. It's mostly when I've been holding hands with Ri that I want to play with Aurie, and I think of Ri the whole time. But when I see Ri, I'm afraid to tell him.

But I do get scared over silly things. Mother says this comes from growing up. But we mustn't think mothers always right.

Ri

In the wind, we ran to the trains and went to the movies. It was a sentimental film, and we held hands. I said,

"It's too dark to see you, and you're so pretty." "Even in the dark," she answered, "you know I'm with you, and I know you're with me." I started to ask what she really thought of me, but I didn't.

Afterward, we walked around downtown, petting alley cats and watching the people in the Senlo tenements, but the soldiers pushed everyone back while they "made an arrest." A crowd of guys began to throw rocks at them, and I wanted to, too, but I had Maia, a girl, along. Instead, we crossed the square to the bus—they had closed off the Underground—while soldiers in gasmasks watched us. A boy about our age had just been shot. I said, "Maia, be brave, you're brave," and was so worried for her. On the bus, she kept staring, so I put my arm around her until she leaned her head on my chest and closed her eyes.

It felt so different from anything else; there was a good kind of pride, and I told her about this, so she would talk and not be so far away. She seemed sad, so we began discussing serious things, and I told her why I question the usual concepts of morality, and she mostly agreed. But then she began speaking about her "intuitive knowledge" of guilt.

For some reason, maybe because she was so quiet, I knew I must argue against this concept. I tried to show her that "intuition" can come from selfish fear, but she said, "Don't—let's not talk." When we got off to walk up the hill, she pulled her scarf around her face and began to cry.

Possibly it was the soldiers, I thought. But she took my

hands and said, "I want to tell you something." She was standing still, like the trees behind her, and I realized she might be scared because she wanted to say she likes me. But all she said was, "Do you think Aurie is good?"

I said, "I think he's stupid." I didn't say his ideas are usually false and he betrays friendship, but she wasn't listening anyway. I said, "Tell me what you started to," but my voice shook. She started walking and wouldn't hold my hand.

Maia

Aurie thinks I'm chicken, and snotty like other girls. Only, I did not know that is what we were doing, until Ana showed off that book in class. Then I was too afraid to tell Ri.

I agree with Ri. We mortals with our selfish fears cannot know right and wrong. Only, my fears aren't selfish. I only fear not seeing Ri.

And I keep thinking about that book. I told my mother I am not very good. She said, "That's false. You're very kind to people, that's what counts." Which made me feel better. I should make her a present tonight.

Only, I *have* to make things better with Ri. If I say anything, now—like yesterday, down by the creek—he won't listen. It's because I started to tell him about Aurie, only I was afraid. Now if Ri holds me, it's not like before. He looks intense, and his hands touch in that way, and I get afraid to ask him anything. Even, to speak.

Ri

I thought Maia was tired of me. But two days ago, we were in her living room and I told her my new ideas, why we *do* have to question our knowledge of God. And I said, "After all, we think we have intuitive knowledge of guilt, like you claim, when we're simply afraid."

She looked pale; she said, "You mean, *selfishly* afraid."

"No. Just afraid—any sort of afraid."

That made her jump, and "Oh, of course!" she said. "I should have seen that too." She looked very serious— then, "Listen. I have to tell you something. Now."

I held her hand to keep us calm, and she said, "I feel so good when Aurie and I play. Sometimes we wrestle." She still looked serious.

So I said, "Well, of course. Playing *and* wrestling feel good." I squeezed her hand so she'd laugh too. It must have been the right answer; we kissed for an hour.

This afternoon, I found four flowers by the Haunted Boulder; it made her eyes go cloudy when I put them in her hair.

She said, "I was afraid you wouldn't respect me," I told her I'll always respect her; I said she's the only person I've ever respected. I want her to feel safe. But I still do not understand why we got so afraid; we both risk truth.

Then, I said too much. The only thing I didn't say was she's the only person I've really loved. I said, "Don't you be afraid," but what I have no right to say is "*Do you love me?*"

Maia

Ri just laughed. Maybe someday we'll get married! And I won't have to see Aurie anymore.

I should be kinder to Aurie. He is unhappy. Ana's book upset him too. Only, he does *not* respect people. He told his friend Steffan about us, after I said I wouldn't play anymore. I told him he better shut up. I threatened him with his paperweight. I pointed out he never cares whether anything's wrong because he never *thinks*.

Only, thinking's not enough. "Be brave," I told myself, but I couldn't tell Ri *everything*. I'm still afraid and we still can't touch right. Instead, I say, "Come on, let's go do something." Then Ri looks away, as if it never happened, what he said by the creek that made me happy. Like last night, on the porch—he got up and left me to follow. We were halfway to the shortcut before he'd speak.

By then, I was acting "like a girl," he said—getting bothered by brambles and later by the sticky vines outside the Base. We saw one long building by the barracks, with barred windows, that he said must be where they keep the prisoners. I was too unhappy to pay attention. But I wasn't afraid of the Base; I'm no coward.

"Imagine what it's like in there," Ri whispered. He said he knows people who "certainly ought to hear about this place." But he looked strange after he spoke; I think he hadn't wanted to remind me about my cousin. He was angry—not at me. We turned around carefully. He didn't take my hand, back on the road. "Do you understand those f----s?" he said. "What is their purpose?"

Ri

Their parents never take them to the beach, so Aurie and Maia were glad to come with us last weekend. In the train, we kept laughing. My mother was happy to be away and not worry about all the arrests; she and my father were getting along, and he even discussed things besides work and his principles.

He took my brother and Aurie fishing when we arrived, and my mother went inside to rest, so I took Maia walking in the surf. I showed her a heron's nest, and we found feathers and dug for crabs. Then, just before dinner, we crossed the dunes and took a rowboat up the inlet to watch the sunset; it was gold, sad light, with dragonflies, like in my old dream, and Maia was happy. She had been mostly silent.

The second night, we stayed out late on the sand after everyone went in, and walked in the whitecaps. We watched the stars and looked for constellations, and I was pointing out Alpha Centauri when I had my insight. If there are beings on planets of other stars, they might be somehow "superior," or of a magnitude beyond our human grasp, and there might be many, many orders of such beings—but, if there are such beings, or even unknowable beings, they might be, even if infinitely more powerful, yet morally "inferior" to us. And therefore—and this has incredible importance for all moralities and meanings of life—why should we call one such possible being "God"? And I didn't mean only that "it" might be *unknowable*, as I'd been thinking lately, but that maybe "it"—"God"—is just a hypothetical idea and doesn't fit anything.

Maia thought this an important insight, too. We were both excited about these ideas, and we felt free for the first time in so long. Maia walked down to where the waves were breaking on the rocks, and I followed, and she said, "You know, I'm not afraid of anything when I'm where you are."

I am sure that's what she said. What I did was, when she said that, I knelt down—the sand was wet—and, as if joking, but I wasn't, kissed her hand. I told her she can always trust me; I told her she was brave. I said, "Please don't be afraid."

We came back to the city the next day. I know Maia trusts me, whether or not she loves me. And maybe she does. The first time I said I loved her—by the creek—it made her look embarrassed, but the second time, there in the surf, she looked happy. I thought, "You're everything there is."

Maia

Aurie says we weren't friendly at the beach. He says Ri used to be his friend. Then Aurie called me a "snot" and sat there, surrounded by his model planes, and said we must have been doing awful things. I said, "We were talking. About serious things. Not like with you."

Because it's Ri who has real things to say. And courage—real courage. Like going to that Youth Camp even though he hates those places. When he gets back, we'll sit out on the grass, and I will tell him everything, not be afraid or make him get afraid. He respects me, he loves me, he'll laugh and say, "You *can't* still believe that received morality!" and "Silly, it's all right."

Three days more until he gets back. I can be brave that long. *And then I* will *tell you.* I swear it, on this heron plume we found.

Ri

It isn't true. They've wired my father to come get me; they've got the big guys in to keep me down; I can't get out. I struck that guy Steffan, that liar; I went wild. He's twice my size, and I beat him into the ground.

But that doesn't change it.

I'll burn down the tents. I'll spit on the priest. Just let me out.

But I still can't get away from the truth.

No. She *loves me.* She said, "I'm not afraid when I'm with you."

Not this.

Maia

My mother made me come shopping, and I cried in the store. Aurie keeps whispering weird things and locking me out of his room.

I saw Ri's father bringing him home. They wouldn't let anyone in. Then Ri came to the window. He shouted "Keep away" until they made me leave.

I wanted to talk about everything. I waited so long. I'm scared again. Ri will not leave his room, they say.

Ri

Thursday was the worst, or yesterday. If things would stop changing for five minutes, I could kill myself. But that wouldn't stop it. If what Mik said is false, I'm dirt to believe it. But if it's true, then she lied, she couldn't have loved me, reality is upside down.

No, I think Steffan lied. I'll see Maia, we'll just hold hands, there's nothing to ask. But what's good in me trusts her. Yet if I did trust her, I would ask.

I saw them together; I fooled myself. But then why did she say she felt so beautiful with me? But it doesn't matter—this is the worst: if I think of asking her, or if I think of them together, it's as if I, too . . . No, it doesn't matter what the truth; I cannot see her anymore.

In what anyone has done or felt, there is no evil. Only symbols, as if to comfort her. But whatever we had is gone. And I know, now: what "I" want is good, but there is no "I"—not since I started thinking I loved Maia. We and "our love" were unreal.

We thought we knew our way around this universe. We thought we were so free. But we are nothing, no one.

Maia

I need to see Ri. He was outside, last week, and I did not know what to say (because he's been hitting people and they say he might be crazy). I asked was he better now (I *said* that!)

He said, "Keep away. Don't touch me." He said that he was late, but he can't be going to school. They threw him out. His eyes were slits.

Mother is sending me to stay with Aunt Elena for awhile. I will have singing lessons there.

Ri

Too bad, I told that tyrant, I'm not tame anymore; I don't believe in those things. We are what we have to be. No more "truth-seekers"—children in a tinsel dream. The people I meet now know these things. That pretty Tralee keeps laughing, and she makes me laugh, she's so funny, but she sells herself to feed her kid and she has no hopes. The guys downtown, too, know there's nothing else. It is a lie to think that anyone accepts the emptiness inside; but if this is the world, okay—I like it here.

Maia

I gave my mother the news from Aunt Elenka, and changed my clothes and walked up to Gold Creek. There were leaves on the ground, but I didn't feel anything. I sneaked up to Ri's room just because I *am* a sneak. The room's all changed around.

Ri lay in bed—like *drunk*. Aurie says Ri gets in trouble

all the time, downtown. Now Aurie's scared of him, now Aurie's got a "respectable" job.

Ri looked annoyed. He said, "You want to climb in? You've become a very peripatetic young lady."

I ignored the insult; I don't know what he really meant—if anything. I sat on the floor and talked about my cousins. I showed Ri a leaf from the creek. He looked away. I started to take his feathers down from the shelves, just to touch something. Then he slapped my hand.

And stood up. He said, "I'm not drunk, Maia," and started crying. I did, too. I wanted to tell him how stupid my old fears seem, and what I think really happened. I wanted to say, "Ri, please don't you be scared, don't hurt anymore"—but how can one gloat that way? I mean, it may be me who did this.

Ri handed me the feathers. He said, "Here are some new ones." We spread them on the floor. I sat beside him and looked at them. He kept touching my hand with one feather. I did not know what to say. I whispered, "You told me to always trust you. I do." He said, "I didn't want you to be afraid." It was hard to hear. I was still scared, but I asked, "What do you mean?" He said, "No, nothing." Then he said, "You see, it cannot be." He looked at me. "The fault isn't yours. Anyhow, what I am, you wouldn't want. Either that, or life is meaningless."

I said, "Don't say that."

"You don't think life is meaningless? That's good." He hadn't understood.

His hands came near my hair. I reached to wipe his

tears. I had wanted to say "Don't you be afraid." He stared at my eyes and held my palms against his cheeks. Then there started to be electricity, and he said, "Let's not be childish" and pushed my hands away. "I'm at the university. I have to study, you see."

"I wanted to talk with you."

His eyes turned slits again. His mouth looked mean. "You better see. These things are dead."

I said, "Ri." Finally I said, "Be careful. Or they'll catch you guys."

He laughed—not at me. Then he asked, "Hey, you want to make it?" I started to cry again, and he said, "Why don't you wake up?" and faked a sigh. I stepped over to pick up the feathers. He lay back and said, "'Bye. You be very good, now."

I sneaked down the stairs. When I got home, I broke the heron plume. I will tie it together when Ri comes back to me.

Ri

Even four years ago, of course it was too late. That spring, I headed up the action groups, and four of us were hurrying, slipping downtown toward our first mass demonstration, when we heard those steps out of the dark, and—that voice reached my heart—"Ri, I must warn you . . ." That Security was tracking me—could she have thought I didn't know? I was brusque, rude. She was still so pretty; she said, "Ri, it's been years." I said, "Yes, I'll get word to you soon, very soon," but we had to keep moving, we couldn't stop longer, and she knew that, she understood the danger. But it hurt her, I know, that I didn't look at her. We went on down the riverfront, and she turned away, being discreet and brave.

But how could I have seen her, what good could it have done? We had our time; for so many, it has always been too late. Whatever caring I have learned can never fill the people's hopelessness and need, but if the struggle in Serenidad can't break the myths that trapped myself and Maia once, it may—must—end our people's greater misery.

And what could I tell Maia now? It happened; we loved; we fell into the world.

These evenings in the meetings, I try to give a little comfort and we propagandize, we wait in these rooms. And when the thoughts return—but no longer each few minutes, breaking and changing the universe—I do not try to understand.

November

At the end, Millie told us, he had said, "'Come outside—listen how the crickets are singing!'" and taken her hand. Her fingers had trembled. The rain had been clearing, the stars brilliant; "I cannot forget." Leaning on her creaky garden fence, he'd said, "You told me, once, you discovered, through your antiwar actions, that you cared for many and your love was whole—that you could live again." He was glad for her, he'd said, had never meant to hurt her; "Only, understand, Mil"—he'd spread his fingers in an open, quiet gesture—"for me, it is too late."

Too late—she'd heard the words re-echo. Without thinking, she had stretched her left hand toward his forehead, as if about to bless him. "Only, it was I who'd been in love with him, not he with me; I did not dare. And then I felt his hand across my forehead, blessing me. I don't know how long we stood there. Then he was gone."

Millie sat silent, staring into the gold lamplight. We too were silent. I think it must have been at this time we began to recognize—though still decades before the first collapse—how old (and now brief) our lifetimes had become.

A Tale of the Sixties

And how would you form fiction from an era when every action held a new, felt truth and widened meaning? Especially if such truth or meaning has again real import for our lives?

Far easier to speak these truths, of course, had one been able to retain the pristine voice of someone never trapped by falsifying voices and constructions of some earlier time. But as things stand, or stood, consider this. Should you have wished—or wish today—to write a "real life" story of, for instance, childhood trauma—ostracism, say, in twentieth-century U.S. schools—you would research (have researched) children of an inner-city playground, look(ed) inside the classrooms of the Great Depression, study (studied) a one-room rural schoolhouse—not (have) start(ed) from the narrow viewpoint of some socially backward, "intellectual" child of one particular early Cold War generation whose "normal" females were expected to be plumply rounded, white, with yellow curls, and any difference was seen as lesser. No, you would study, instead, the kids who most clearly fought back, who did t not simply stand alone, year after year on the playground, "unpopular." You'd look for kids whose rebel instincts shone, not for a blundering shy naïve who'd, all too soon, be sheltering her wakening sexuality while seeking (if with adolescent, clichéd ignorance) "The Truth"—of life, of love, philosophy—oblivious that such a goal would lead but to a campus life of groping sex, repetitive debate, and competition that must precisely target the natural and curious, body and mind.

Or, what if you had—let's just suppose—concocted a cool, albeit cornball, fiction along these lines? Surely you'd have built some strong—nobly witty, wittily noble—young protagonist, heroic really, certainly not a late-adolescent nervous, "serious-minded" female unable to cover emotion enough to hide her love away and thus reel in her man. Surely instead you'd build a brash, brave tomboy of a flirt—a Katniss or a Vida—whom all men must desire, not some frail, compulsive, male-adoring "chick" who suffers multi unrequited loves before meeting those who, as your "late-'60s" masculine characters, become her erstwhile lovers.

Hey and look, above all, never would you link your would-be masterpiece to that Fanon-like slogan of those times, "Oppression means to think 'What's wrong must come of something wrong in me.'" Especially since, on our combustible crowded Earth amid today's new horrors, any insistence that internalized oppression could be basic seems not only seriocomic but damned dumb.

Yet was it? For, what must be said, of that decades-long forced self-destruction that finally the "'60s" ended, is this: what was wrong, in those early years—a period when even someone too sophisticated to swallow popular Freudian-isms might be swallowed by them—was seen as deeply wrong indeed. What was wrong was seen ("in yourself, babe, 'cause it ain't my doing") as dangerous, dark, some underlying twist or dearth in one's basic human feelings, mind, or (especially) sexuality. A venerated professor might slight a provincially dressed woman's arguments for iden-tical statements from a well-coiffed, sleek bohemian, but it was everyone—venerated or provincial—who took with utmost seriousness society's cautions about "sick, aggres-sive, possessive" women and found frigid whoever failed to "come" as "came" the characters of D. H. Lawrence. It was, early in this present tale, a closeted young man adored by our protagonist who took her tremorous hand but soon, unable to enter her, blamed their sexual failure on her "cas-trating vagina"—and it would be she herself, a year later, who followed the theories denouncing—in a time when "disability rights" would only have met laughter—her love for a scarred man as necessarily perverted. Again, this (or any) protagonist, questioning her admiration for a gutsy younger woman as "probably perversion," would have taken seriously, too, suggestions she try psychotherapy if— gangly, Jewish, thin, a slow typist—she couldn't get hired.

But "again," as this protagonist might have said (and, shortly, let us call her "I," as if our tale were memoir)—as "she" well might have said to her ("my," "our") child, "these experiences were standard. The webs of self-condemnation, the equation of failure or weakness with 'regressed personality,' of sexual or economic 'success' with 'maturity,' and of maturity with 'the capacity to truly love,' meant few folks in those years could have considered themselves whole and have not believed, like Fanon's colonized, 'I must first change what's wrong in me before I can—really—judge, live, love.'"

And people fell for this—as indeed our protagonist might, now, add—who, in other areas, knew better—"even we who questioned bomb shelters, segregation, national security, and saw past the commonplaces, religious to relativist, of the times. For, though we questioned"—she (this "I") would (will) add—"we failed to formulate the obvious challenges—observing, for example, the teleological absurdity and daily drudgery of parenthood, yet ignoring the related denigration of life—of children, old people, the mother-infant bond."

After all, she (this "I") might (may) yet, in our world, tell her ("my") grown, politically conscious son, "When the world's inside out, it took little intellectual slippage to fall into mirror-land." And oft we fell. Until, one day . . .

Here, her/our story begins.

Summer of '65, another fifty thousand troops heading off to Vietnam, and in Berkeley I had been working (because, however trivial might be "meaningful" activity or dubious my inner motives, still it was necessary to counter massacre) with something called the Citizens' Committee Against the War—I answered the door to an older, dark-eyed man from another country. He was radical beyond my experience. He respected and cared for people in a way I'd never known. I came to love him. One afternoon—he had been away—he visited unexpectedly.

Afraid that trying to hide response must seem defensive, I offered myself. ("I want you." Did I believe something wrong in my love, to risk—to give up—so much on those three words?) But he reached out his hand—"It's all right."

Only, it wasn't—because my offer was sexual but the love was deeper. I didn't know if he acceded from kindness, but I sensed something and, between this hesitance and the old body-doubting fear not to open, I held back, said "Wait" (a strange—laughable?—request, even today, in such circumstances, but then self-perceived as unspeakable, unwomanly). Sensitive, not like men of this country, he stopped. I never learned what he thought. Much later he said he had missed me and "There are no judges. But also you must let me be my way."

The next weeks, waiting, I broke into ricocheting bits. "Let's just be natural," he had told me; I came to think it my sexual inhibitedness that had failed him. Something must have, surely, since he did not return yet could only have shown such care if he loved—unless his was an all-encompassing love beyond my comprehension. Not to judge meant to trust in his return, to make no judgment of what was true, no decision what to do. Any judgment came of a system of rational artifice, suspicion and doubts of love from precisely that life-destroying system we opposed.

It was not, finally, only the one afternoon, the one man, but the shadows of my whole past led me, the next three weeks, through the two surging crests of stunned belief—the first, that even the hesitance of my body and proclamation of desire were meant to entice and sacrifice the beloved to those (parts of "myself," the superego "parents", as it were) who judged—but the second, that I'd not such an inner demand for sacrifice but rather clung like a child to love for some (interiorized) parent and thus, in a sort of transference, to the unreal needs and unattainable loves defined by elders' judgments and words. My one hope was to regrow a truer self, experience what I'd never known, that I might find new ways to care, to—nonjudgingly, maturely, really and all-encompassingly—love.

But I can't further explain how that not uncommon experience of loss and the ideas of that period led to this conclusion, or how, for so many of us, the evolving external events and concepts—spontaneity, play, distrust of systemic judgments—cross-fertilized (abetted by the culture's hidden demand to "learn lessons") internal query and change. What is important is that interwoven with the confusion and denial were truths.

My son would have appeared immediately to understand this, those first weeks of our reunion, but not today.

How can one era know the cultural mazes of another—but also there was his need, after our re-bonding, to re-separate. And perhaps a fear that there might have been only some casual "summer of love" came to shadow his at first exhilarated words, "I used to think—Berkeley, 1967, maybe the radical scene was involved." So that, now as then, I would say "Yes, you were borne, child, on something very deep."

In any case, it's not only to my now-grown child that I'd continue, "The quest for meaning, universal love, and peace may be old, but to meld this search with the climb from under psychological oppression began, for so many of us, what was a revolution; our antiwar acts also sought new identity, new forms. It was not that we joined the Movement 'to work out [supposed] patholo-gies,' but rather our involvement in the ever-growing need for peace of a country at war, our search for new ways to care in a society of frozen compassion, forced us to evolve—strand by strand, and often threaded with mistakes—larger tissues of structure and self."

Yet this now seems clichéd. It was too fragile then.

So, to "use my words for others, not to express false 'personal problems,'" I turned to antiwar reporting. At that time, this meant the *Berkeley Barb*—no focus of compassion, but one of only four antiwar papers in the nation. It was a base from which to both reach the people exploring new ways and to meet the urgent need—every day on the news were the photographs—to oppose the war, to stop the massacre, save lives.

I was writing the events column ("Sat 3 pm Lincoln Brig dinn; Fri 8 pm Avalon, Jeff Air"—*Barb* tending to tight spacing) and reporting on the peace movement. It was thus as a reporter in that spring of antiwar actions, amid appalling rumors that Johnson would soon bomb Hanoi, that I met the macho peace activist who, for a few weeks, became the father of my first child. There was love, on my part—and over that next month we found we could have arguments, even be silly, even disagree without making the other go away. Yet there were tacit limits; I must avoid judging, never ask "false needs" or fall into "unreal closeness," and he—Dave—could not drop his taut self-image of focused challenge against the war. Thus we never discussed that "System's" self that is biography; everything was of the moment, only the body and emotions connected.

"But they did," I'd say; "Dear child, they did."

After four weeks, though, Dave and I began to laugh more, open more—and of course at that point he was gone. Twice in the next weeks, I stood on the sidelines as he addressed a Berkeley rally, the crowd cheering his daring, funny antiwar actions. By then, this country had bombed Hanoi and Haiphong, and that day the pregnancy been confirmed.

"Therapeutic" abortions existed—one had only to adjust; I had still the requisite contacts and self-doubts. My struggle for renewal precluded asking parental help, and, like most middle-class women, I was ignorant of Welfare.

Meanwhile, I'd had threatening phonecalls and my fear, called "paranoid" by *Barb* coworkers (COINTELPRO was unknown), seemed clearly to show I was still trapped in "self"-protective closure and judgment and thus must question "my" decisions. Yet finally the outcome was never in question; it came down to life, to giving (even though to have a man's baby might seem symbolic possession), to love for the growing life within.

I would have the child. I would give up the child. (I'd known a few who had, just as I'd known those who had aborted; it was what one did, and went on.) Neither I nor anyone else could regard this matter as so important as the struggle against the war.

Around this time, someone came to the *Barb* with word of a demonstration planned for the military base at Port Chicago. This was a man named Tom, who showed me what it is to risk one's life from love, and who knew to reach through fear and anger, to listen and be vulnerable, to speak of his need for me—so that I came to see I could love and had always loved and been whole, and to glimpse the strength of a world where people trust their own love's possibilities.

(Once my son asked, because I had mentioned the event several times, "What happened at Port Chicago?" but I could only relate the episode, not its crucial effects. Besides, words, in the first weeks of reunion, emerge slowly from shared depths).

The demonstration began in early August with a

march to the Port Chicago/Concord Naval Weapons Station, shipping point for the bulk of American weapons to Vietnam. There, protestors would block the weapons trucks, however briefly—by this nonviolent civil disobedience focusing attention on the war. Tom was among the leaders even though, like many of us, he questioned the tightly structured limits of the action. I had begun to know him well—this big, gruff, army veteran who was always aiding people, who had promised to help me through my pregnancy, who intuited the core of issues— and to whom, only partly from having lived in Korea, the Vietnamese were not vague victims but persons who must be saved. During long talks, I had tried to explain my changes, he to recount a lonely past. "We all need to be like children," he would say. "Children are curious about everything, they care about everyone."

Outside the base that first night, across from what was called Main Gate, few remained. We slept fitfully. Only with dawn came the trucks, and—as one after another protestor stepped out to nonviolently halt their onrushing approach—a new, "impossible" form of community, a love for, and through, each other. I understood this, when Tom put his hand on one brave woman's shoulder; I felt his care for her, our love for her and one another—even perhaps for those lounging Marines across the road, certainly even for the distant, unknown people in Vietnam.

But after Tom was arrested, I—pregnant, afraid, trying not to judge but still skeptical of strict civil disobedience—only carried the tapes and photos to the press.

In the next days, a separation began between those arrested and those not, between those constantly on the lines—as what became a vigil continued—and "new people." Out there only occasional nights, I became distanced from Tom.

Meanwhile, over several days the vigilers' numbers shrank, and the danger from the Marine guards, sheriff's deputies, and local hecklers grew.

So we came to "that night," I told my son, "August 16-17, 1966." A few well-known activists had responded, in Washington, to subpoena by the House Un-American Activities Committee with widely publicized agit-prop. A rally had been called in Berkeley to back them, and that hot night the crowd in the stifling auditorium quickly moved also to support the vigil. Two young ABC television reporters were there, and people were encouraged by the media presence, the challenge to HUAC, the intense commitment at Port Chicago; at the speakers' crescendoing calls, they swarmed outside, moving by carloads toward the vigil in the night.

I didn't go in the van with Tom. By then, I didn't dare; it was "their scene," they'd been "out there." Instead, I guided a bunch of "new people" to the base.

Suddenly, Tom was running toward me; we held each other, across from Main Gate on the roadside strip of grass.

But it was only for a moment, and soon he moved off. In spite of his doubts, "If we keep coming back and stopping the weapons," he had begun to insist, "more people will see it's possible—they'll see they can care, and will come—and we can close this base and we can stop this war"; with the crowds—and publicity to bring more—finally arrived, it was necessary to act. Besides, the sudden upsurge had maddened the hecklers, and "Tom, we need you over here," some vigiler cried out.

Without glancing back, he went loping up the slope to the crest of the road. Soon I could see him standing there with several others, by the triangle of dirt formed by what was called the Overpass Road turnoff. Here, the weapons trucks slowed to enter the base, and here, clearly, people planned to stop them. As I walked hesitantly up the hill, an older pacifist shouted "You know the scene. Tell any new people the rule—if someone goes out to stop a truck and is attacked, no one is to try to protect them, it'll only make things worse." I nodded, and recalled I must not judge.

There was a long wait. Near the triangle of ground, Tom and the other vigil veterans—the fragile-looking legal secretary Pamela, the tough farm mother Jo, the Barb's cynical photographer Eliot, one or two others— stood apart, beside the two young men who planned to stop the night's trucks; their quiet voices now and then rose as they planned tactics. Nearby, the television crew sat, smoking cigarettes. Across the way, Marines and police lounged in taut silence. Only occasionally Eliot would wander over to where I waited, isolated between the "in" group and the line of vigilers stretching down to the massed "new people" across from Main Gate.

Sometime after midnight, someone pointed. Five yellow lights were approaching—a truck, coming in from Concord. Behind it, another five lights. Both vehicles were moving fast. Very fast.

As the first rushed up the hill, still accelerating, the two young men raced out to meet it—and jumped back; it was coming too fast. In a moment, it had made its turn and rushed on, napalm bombs gleaming, into the base. Then—again, too fast—the second truck appeared.

Someone, in the television lights, was running toward it. In that moment, I saw it was Tom, his arms lifted, and that the person would be killed. And if I ran out, I and the baby might also die—or I might confuse his timing, increase his danger, and was I trying to possess him?

The road at my feet in the light shone white. Something, the truck, was passing. If I took one step, he, someone (—I couldn't see, was it Tom? I'd not liked how the person held his arms—) might be killed, I might be hurt, the baby, these people, everyone might be hurt—and he might not want me there, it would intrude upon his scene, his courage—he was the one who cared, who could love; I'd only make things worse. . . I don't recall the exact thoughts, but then the truck had passed.

The demonstrator had not been killed, but the Marines had pulled him down, were striking him, and if I took one step—

Someone—Pamela—had raced forward and was tearing at the nearest Marines, breaking through their lines.

As she and the others brought Tom back, in the white television lights the people's hands were raised in V-signs and their voices sang "We Shall Overcome." "Now I am dead," I thought. "Now I shall never overcome."

Later—Pamela and Tom were still by the turnoff, each insisting on stopping the next truck—I said, "I'll stop the next one" but no one heard. As I turned away, Eliot came over; together we walked down the hill "to find a ride before," as he expressed it, "someone gets himself killed."

There was another wait, standing around with the newcomers by the food table, before Eliot wandered back, saying "I've found a car; let's go." I nodded, glancing up. Beyond him, down the road, were five yellow lights.

"Truck," I said. "Truck, Eliot, truck."

He was trying to put film into his camera. The lights kept coming nearer; he said, "Run—go put your arms around him or something—run."

I did (I'll always know I didn't run out before that truck). Then Tom and Pamela and Jo were moving toward it, and I could see Marines immediately grabbing the women and throwing them back. For a second the load of bomb-crates blocked the light, then it was past. The scene had repeated. Tom lay cordoned off by Marines.

But this time it was like a dance, my feet could move, and I ran across the road.

Only, for a long time there was no way through. Once a Marine grabbed me and Jo and pushed us toward the base. But we fought, my sandal strap broke, the Marine—he was very young—let go. I kicked off my shoes and ran back towards Tom. But no way opened; for so long we swayed there, lines in silent confrontation; then suddenly two Marines stood in the light, one was black and one was white, and then there was a space. I ran to Tom.

I leaned over him—"They'll have to hit me first," I thought, but told him only "We're here." I heard him say "I'm alright." I knew he mustn't move his injured leg, yet I feared the Marines' return.

But they had pulled back, the demonstrators had got through. Everything was safe.

And then abruptly the security guard's halfton truck rolled toward us from the base. But no one expected danger, everyone jumped aside; only I, standing by Tom's head, was still in its way. I didn't see how I could help him—hold onto the hood and push him sideways with my feet, possibly—but somehow I would; I stood between him and the little truck, while its headlights approached within inches, and then it stopped. "My feet," (as I've said, too often, of this), "took root."

"Sure must have—she hasn't left the '60s since," one might say, and were this a memoir, not a tale, one would have to add "and some have." But it was to the changes and—though I did not understand—to the child, I have clung. Again, were this a memoir, here one would add, "We were still in the wonder of reunion when I told my son of that night."

It was not solely this one night (and the earlier morning's "impossible" community of love) that formed for me (*notes our protagonist, this "I"*) the crucial metaphor of "getting through"—of fighting past the bars of one's own and others' fears, shames, guilts, denials, to the love and strength in everyone—this metaphor for both personal or intimate love and a more loving, "order"-less society. This metaphor—or new comprehension—came, too, or even mostly, from recognizing the deep response of my love when Tom, over the next two months, would say he needed me—and from the love for the baby growing in my womb.

And what became clear during this time (even as Tom, caught up in the vigil where I could no longer go, slowly left me), the message of this metaphor, was that my—everyone's—love had always been whole and real and simply love. There was nothing wrong or unreal in feelings or self. The feared aggression was a way to fight for people (even words or judgments might be tools), to struggle through barriers (even those of words, of judgments, of denial) to help where one may care. The feared empathy for a man who is vulnerable (it was still the wake of the 1950s, the moment before "women's liberation," and this idea novel) was simply tender response, was even desire to renew the wholeness and strength in the beloved and receive his giving love. The terrifying "possessiveness" was only the struggle of concern. The deepest need—in a person laughing, in a person weeping, in a lost beloved, in a calling child—was the same; the cry to be loved and the murmur of love's offer were one voice, "child's need" and "giving, mature" love not distinct, for each yearned, in one's depths, to give love; this deepest need, the love for the love, in everyone yearned for this same love in each.

But in this truth lay also the possibility of peaceful anarchy, the natural "good life"—for to know one's depths are love, and one's worth thus unbreachable, is to step beyond fear into revolutionary hope, reaching out with curiosity and courage to care, no longer held back by barriers of doubt or interdiction, by the guilts or shames from any eyes, denials of any systems, but letting love lead—even through actual lines of cops, of Marines, of those who kill—together in the struggle to create a world of peace and the possible dream.

I know—again what once seemed liberating sounds parody or trite. There is no way now, after fifty years to make intellectually convincing the wonder, the awareness (unexpected, for the struggle then was against oppression, not for—or from—philosophical "answers") that everything—the beautiful, the good, the natural—could merge in the love that was most deep. Especially when these newly opened eyes could be blind to what was clear.

For, while mine may have been a homespun "woman's definition of love," (influenced, as well, two years before the women's movement, by Helen Lynd's book *Shame and the Search for Identity*), I had not yet enough seen through the dominant climax-oriented version, with its insistence on the emotional primacy of lovemaking and its tacit paradigm of maturity as the "couple" with kids. I could not fully believe the deepest love was equally the agapé, the heroic, even the bond (I could not see, child,) between parent and newborn that—growing, speaking in my soul but the words uncomprehended—hovered those months when the baby's heart met mine and perhaps I cried his cries and dreamed his dreams and (as later in the time of our re-bonding) it was not only hope from new *concepts* brought euphoric joy.

This is, of course, also the love that bears the faith to raise a child.

But early in 1967, six months after Port Chicago, eighteen months after Watts, one week after the first Be-In, when the baby was born I, like my "vanguard" peers, still thought love for a child must be secondary and a baby needed the love of a two-parent home. When I held my newborn close, feeling nothing but tenderness, decision had already been made; besides, the mental struggle against the years' losses and against the sorrow yet to come occluded the simple recognition I'll be giving my baby into the unknown.

And so it was remainders of ignorance and shreds of loss—not simply circumstance, not only the insecurity of "How could I raise such a wonderful child?" or folklore of the perfect, carefully selected, adoptive parents—made the decision; the hope, the belief, was also too frail and new. Yet "I remember," I told this child, "how you flew into the doctor's hands. Three times, I held you. One day Tom sat beside us, showing me the way to make silk god's-eyes. How tiny you looked in that yellow-tiled nursery, the noontime I left."

The radios were playing "Strawberry Fields Forever" and "Ruby Tuesday"; soon it was "Somebody to Love." At the agency, I wouldn't sign until they brought "the baby," and I rocked him—bigger, older, *different*. When he cried, the worker lifted him out of my incompetent hands . . . with which I signed the papers, thinking everyone unnecessarily emotional, and, through the next months, wove the little god's-eyes, like booties to protect a child-idea.

Afterwards I lived two years "as if" (something like the Movement's "as if" to create a better world by believing it)—"as if" there would be response, "as if" would come the loving need, as if by acting "as if" with love I might again care, by reaching find "someone out there." I marched with a hundred thousand in the April Mobilization, leafleted the docking *Enterprise*, organized *Barb* workers, helped to build the Peace and Freedom Party, stood before the cops at Stop the Draft Week, at People's Park. . . . And there were efforts toward two shaggy men; there were an agit-prop, a fledgling women's group, a collective-run magazine. But the crest was over, and perhaps it was as if I could never have been giving enough, no matter how much I gave, and, like so many—and was this one reason our revolution ebbed too soon?—had given everything away.

By the end of another decade there would be another love, another child; I put the god's-eyes in the trunk. My son's new parents would indeed be parents—loving, doting, protecting him in the sensitivity of a good childhood. The truths—the trust that one can love, the recognition that love and our trust in it may heal the world—would hold firm. And the self-acceptance and internal changes, the loves of those days, the care and heroism of Port Chicago, "revolutionary hope" itself, and social progress of those times were crucially important and deep.

Only, in clearing out the layers of false voices and destructive systems of this false society—in finding in the world and self what was loving, life-protective, motherly, and coming to brief revolutionary (so to speak) fruition—somehow that theoretical-minded, "giving" young woman I was had made a big mistake—I had thrown out the baby with the bath water.

"The changes and commitment of 'those days' were real," I *(that is, our protagonist—and now you, too)* will conclude. "Yet the loss and yearning, unrecognized in that culture and veiled as mere curiosity or aimless seeking even in our dreams, lingered, colored the world; and it was only when you found me—you, son who'd the courage to dare the impossible search—that fear's occlusions could lift and the joy of our reunion spring forth, for the necessary time, from the heart's deepest need, the love that is the depth and hope of human life."

Sentience

A tale of the future

All this happened before the Interstellar Manifest in Recognition of each world-born sentience.

We were still young. I was Parna's female cultural attaché on conquered Lanos, new to Erigan's soaring towers and the work. I loved the silvered skies, bold golden clouds, white waves. Garando was (surprisingly, as masculine Erigis there on Lanos are generally sombre like our own) a striking, gold-furred, brilliant creature, fluent in eight worlds' languages, communicator in each verbal, empath, warbler mode. Someone who had known and suffered much, my lithe and learned good friend and mentor in those months. So wondrous he was, Garando, as we trekked the blasted Flith peaks over Yomba, clambered rock shores to the ancient sculptures of the

Isle of Lan, wandered torn museums where he helped me comprehend Erig traditions, and by evening leaned, sleek head to golden breast and toes to claws, together in the silent rail-ride back to Erigan. I trembled beholding his dark warmth, longed to stroke soft fingertips along that tawny pelt, sense feathery feelers on my skin, his swift thoughts in my soul.

And he, self-trancing on my "innocence," yearned deep—I now know—too.

Remember, this was Parna-years before the Lanos Rising and resultant worlds-wide revolutions that, arising from the Seekers Movements of the 2460s, gave each sentience a sense of trusted self to freely seek out love. We were afraid.

"Hold me, beauty," Garando's tongue out-flicked. His fur misted my palms, his feelers coiled my arms. We rode the lift, gilt air below pricked by the darkened spires of Erigan. We wrapped together, heating, swarming dark electric. Squeezed at last into a narrow broken corridor, and through that copper-inlaid door, and lay upon his ivory warm-bed. Silver Moon glowed over Needle.

So few sentiences dared cross species then; I did not understand. He licked my eyelids; bathed in musk-scent, we sought new joy. Who could know a male Eregi needs, to reach a mode to merge a female . . . what, ignorant, I could not give. For hours we squeezed, and yet, even adhering, lay unspent. Until, though shamed by my failure, I dared look up into his orbs.

And he said, "Ah well, beauty, I guess your longing for

the alien arises only from some twist," and added, "I saw a healer once; you must, as well. That you may someday cease to twist an Erig's gift." Yet his feeler stroked my cheek.

I could not doubt him; I left, descending the Thousand Steps. His words had cut a horror of my heart.

Much as our invasion fleets had etched, through that whole millennium, horror into his world. Leaving the puppet caste and upper sex of Lanos to carve Erigis' minds. To teach them doubt of *I* and *Thou*, divide and isolate.

No matter. But it was only through Revolution's changes we could find our own free language and our truths of selves. Only in the years we struggled, together as one—we Parnese, Earthians, Sillas, Erigs, unitd upon Jaranda's barricades, space-trails of old Cortiex and darkest Har—did we learn, in sweat and care and tears, how deep all sentients love. And only then could I come, at last, to see that Garando had been wrong, the "twisting" neither mine nor his but simply concepts foisted in Erigis by our long invasion and their loss, and in we Parnese females by our straitened lives.

I had only, wholly, longed for and loved him.

Now it is another courage needed, an age away on far Sil's sands, knowing what we briefly had and ever lost.

The Other Side of the Pass

Reunion, or the Hole in Time

Number 3—on the door was the large number 3. The woman opened it; I stepped inside.

I said, "You're my kid." He had risen. There were tears in his eyes. My arms had opened; we were holding each other. Shutting the door, the woman said, "Take whatever time you like, we close at five."

He had thick curls now; my hands were stroking them. It was his tears on my shoulders and cheeks.

"I didn't know we'd—"

"What? Be 'stylistically identical'?"

Abruptly we laughed, for two hours we talked and sometimes we laughed, we hugged each other and touched each other's hands and cried. Soon it would be eight hours, sixteen hours, sixty, each tolling and chiming the lost years and new world.

Later I would return to it—his wide-open eyes upon me as we hugged goodbye, the clarity of his profile, feel of his skinny shoulders, warmth of his known long hands—all these fragments calling, burrowing into memory, fastening in so deep the usual content—what was said, the images— seemed lost before the stillness and peace.

The regular world had taken over again—my job, my young teenager—clamoring attention. But later that first evening, when I could lie down and recollect, only bits remained—and the sense of him in heart and womb.

Days alone, I would return to the agency, the long walk with the woman down the corridor, her "Have no expecta- tions" and the people in the lunchroom glancing up, the number 3, the opened door, the lightness of those curls, his chin upon my shoulder and my hands upon his hair.

I showed him pictures. We gave each other pictures. I wrote his telephone number underneath his name. I gave him what I once had made and saved across the years. As if there is a bridge across the years.

The leftover chicken had been sautéed for lunch and I would be driving my teenager to Kids' Connection ("We welcome youth with problems") in an hour. The phone rang; I was beside it, kneeling on the floor.

He said it was he, I said, "Thank God." He said he too had had to work; I said, "I know"; these voices were not our own.

After stopping by Kids' Connection, it was not much longer. Cresting the hill, I saw the park, the fence, some people by the slides and on the grass. Nearer the bridge, he was moving toward me, holding something over his shoulder. *Really he. Really here.* My eyes "found it easier" not to focus; I stretched out my arms.

Our voices had no words. For the next eight hours we would hold each other and cry—on a bench, on a golden lawn. Any doubts, any puzzles, would be left behind. There were two birds on a branch; later I would buy a book to discover they were Steller's Jays. There was the creek below, the light that changed, the sunset—and the fragments, glistening by light so bright, by light that chimed (that seemed to chime; it is the tears and widened pupils create this effect, we know).

This is the tenderness of paradise, the souls remet, the source; this is beyond all other love, is only love.

We were each totally vulnerable.

Beneath the trees and on a curb—another afternoon we clung beneath a staircase in the rain. Later he would give me one portrait so caring it hurt to see. We would query with the voices' slow return. One afternoon he leaned upon my shoulder and I would have kissed the child to sleep. *Where are the years; our arms encircle a peace.*

In between came days to wait, the biding time, the hours of weeping as if reaching in the first days after birth, tenderness turned by waiting to mourning or fear. Learning to remember this person, rediscovering how to move through the pallid furnishings of a changed world—my damaged teenage son, the ordinary jobs and limits—how to make the days pass safely that came between.

I had given this kid up in adoption. This baby, now grown up, had found me.

"My life has been happy so far," he would assure me.

One day he said, "I asked how many found each other there"; I worked the figures in my head—so few. "It's over now," he soothed.

"That expression," he added, "comes close—it was like having a hole, a void, inside."

I could hold him; in the rain beneath the now-old stairs, still wordless in that earlier-than-language, that voice barely mine, surprised by its struggle, had cried "It wasn't that I didn't love you." Conscious he already knew this.

He could hold me. *We really are here.*

There is no knowledge or ritual for this, no understanding of how little in tales or books is true, how wrong the theories of only loss and fear.

When he had phoned the agency, they had located my picture and letter in the file. Those parents had also signed a waiver; by state law of recent years, the rest was not physically hard. Then there was his wait, and for me the corridor, the number on the door.

"No, you were right, I wasn't two weeks old." He'd asked that Mom and Dad. "I'd been in foster care two months."

I said, "I have no picture of your father; photos came

178

of ego, of the system we struggled against—Vietnam, the war. I had none of you until I went back and they gave me this—you, one month old; after ten years, their 'policies had changed.' That day, she left the file out on the desk; I never touched it, I thought, 'That will be up to him, I have no right.'"

Turning awkwardly from his worktable, he said he now found frightening to think of "the randomness," the other possible lives. I exclaimed "But you're the way I'd have you be! It wasn't right, those years you didn't know who . . ."

They say these early hours will pass, like—yet so very unlike—mother and newborn, lovers, myth of the return; they say these hours will pass, the joy and utter vulnerability, with the first harrows of the hole in time. They say one must let go these moments and it is hard; one must let grow the new world. "They say" too much; I mustn't again lose this child to others' fears.

You tell me the adolescent story I once wrote was exactly what you had felt. You see me watching you, ask "What?", and I shake my head and smile or weep. There are already shared humor, remembrances; in the quiet of your living room, we can sometimes even gossip and laugh. But what, in words, this time is for you—what fears or images of other selves, what relocation of your world—I cannot know. Your tears are drying; I would hear you and protect.

It is not right we had not met, not right we must fight for

time to meet. It is not right our love, our rebonding, seems too intense, as if romance, to those who cannot feel the ruptured time—not right time not have been.

Mornings in the office, the sobbing returns. It is as if (I said, "I would die for you") my body cries like a hungry baby calling the vanished mother, cries as you too have cried, in tenderness, *not* separate—not phoning, not wanting to have to trade, for your presence, your respect.

I thought there would be time, time to listen and understand. We have laughed so much, but sometimes your voice is crisp and humor fades. I would tell you to take care, maternally stroke your hair.

We have said, "I know," "I am glad."

The sun-motes fill the room; leaf shadows dance on your walls. The poem was

> Shiver and shake yourself, dear tree,
> and silver and gold rain down to me

in the illustrated *Seven Swans* of my own youth. Childhood is so huge. I would cloak you with glimmer and jewels, would have sung you lullabies.

When you answer "No, come over," I can deny I've heard the change. But change is real; I must let separate, let grow—although I know this child, more swift to descend the mountain, yet would gladly stretch out his hands and is my child and *not* rejecting me; but rather I feel bereft, as when I wakened yearning for my baby after you were gone, this broken love a mourning in the hole in time.

In what depth you must have, then, mourned me.

There are those who are not found.

"You inherited my nervous system"—"Hey, I know." I remember telling you of one demonstration, and your eyes as you heard, and I feel like the little fir tree remembering the attic. I love you so much. Sometimes the tears have been to reach, sometimes from sorrow, sometimes not daring to express the happiness.

But for the tears and joy, the tenderness in the fragmented light of those early hours, care for the vulnerability of these chiming weeks, and afternoons and hours still—blessed those hours, blessed this wood—for the lost return in paradise, the simple love of here, there are no words; there is this deepened, softened, different voice. Blessed be the love.

The years took us far, and in the middle of January, the new war was on, and people dying from our bombs as on our streets, the first big march would happen the next day and then there was the letter ("Some years ago you wrote this agency . . .") in the mailbox.

Very soon the war was over. Then the corridor, the room, the number on the door.

Your picture shows you holding a beautiful cat; you've a shy young adolescent smile; the cat is startled by the light but obviously calmed in your arms. Now you are a man.

You came from my womb in the very early morning, flying out into the doctor's arms. Three times in the hospital I held you; you had already those long fingers and fine features, and your eyes (then dark blue) saw me, *but I cannot be his mother, children need two parents, how could I raise so wonderful a child?* (those very arguments I would "resolve," mistakenly, years later for that other son because finally I "could not do it twice"). Once I held you in a silent room on the courtyard of the agency, a little while and then the time was over and—for you, but over the abyss of chance— I signed the papers. I signed the papers; I signed the papers.

You said, "I remember once when my grandfather . . ." You said, "My Mom used to . . ."

If I start to cry, if you start to cry, your hand, my hand, not very different, is immediately there; in the glance of an eye, "I know."

You look away, leaving "these" (seeking a soft word) "first spaces"—the early unity, the *adoration*—where I remain. Has my slowness to let go been cause, or is this natural return to the pendulum of time? You feared to hurt me by acknowledging your distance sooner; I'd sensed this, child, yet your compassion moves my soul.

Your life has been happy, I know. I am so glad you found me, so thankful you exist, that you are you.

Once, you said, "I do not want to lose you."

The love tears my heart.

On Sabbath

Something, some "scrunch" out there. Probably Cougar hopping up to the flower box, scratching to come in. No matter.

If God is the Omniscient One, how can there be necessity to pray, why need we sanctify this day? For surely, he/she/it already knows our soul.

To Rebecca, tiny figure seated bone-tired yet ramrodstraight beneath the lamp, the long thoughts were as worn as new, part of the Sabbath's heart, jeweled structure of this universe, created by (*whatever this may mean*) God's will.

Created, that is—her fingers spun the space-pen, Judah's parting gift "in token how they tried to break you from your mother-love for me," precisely, once—*by Thine own will alone.*

Thick with embroidery, the white wool robe clung against her shoulders. Her gaunt head, hollow-eyed, sank toward the inlaid writing-table, its thick-stacked pages. These formed a book of prayers, neither leather-bound nor ornately tooled, no more traditional than her unending (Judah's dad used, with that lightning smile, to term them "obsessive") thoughts.

Again, outside, that "scrunch." But no—a "crunch," rather. Not Cougar; Cougar's lithe small paws moved tight and silent, could never scuffle noise across the panes between the garden and the studio wall.

No matter. Prayer, and thought on God, is Sabbath's toil. *Though not,* she wrote, *in any rigorous sense a "needed" toil.* She shoved the heavy sleeves above her beveled bracelets; lifting both thin arms in the disciplined stretch of an aging lioness, she stood on tiptoe, giving thankfulness, then forced her weary body back upon the chair.

Sabbath must, as ever, be observed—though God, since God, need not require prayer as proof of faith.

Therefore she should concentrate—not go to check the windows, not glance toward, beneath the shadowed maple trees, that sound. A yowl? But Cougar was far off, prowling another yard. This was a "tinkle," rather. Glass?

A footstep. Beside her chair.

"Shut your fuckin' lips, bitch." Stinking like cabbage. "Hold still, ya won't get hurt. I need some."

Yet God, since God, requires what God will.

"Hey, look at *me*, bitch. Wanna get cut?"

For, even were "will of God" *pure concept—*

Rebecca's eyes kept to the text, one hand clutching the wet seeping wool.

"Down, cunt." Fingers jerked her robe so she must cease to write. The book spilled off the table, pages awry.

No, he *would* not, this pimply teenaged hunk, this hood, leave her in peace, but he kept shoving his body, sweaty and unclean, in where he should not. Now she'd have again to shower, and tape these wounds.

"Done yet?" Rebecca spoke precisely, brooking no contradiction. "Let me alone, child." She had raised, those years after Judah's birth, three more. (So beautiful, they'd been.)

Not cabbage—spoiled onions, this hood; his glazed eyes blinked. "Shit, ma'am, I'll help ya straighten, here."

They never meant their messes. "Just go."

There were departing footsteps—muffled, creaking to a run. Then Cougar's pressing head and purring body leaned against her ankles. Her hand, allowed to tremble now, reached down to stroke his warmth. Broken, that window would become a regular expressway—raccoons and possums, too.

Or the stinky boy return. She'd best get up, bring in a sheet of plywood from the shed, and barricade the empty space. Yet this would mean to care again for all that was—caring enough to lose yet more crowned moments to prevent intrusion on (*why do we still, in our awareness, say?*) Sabbath toil, Sabbath grace.

Chinking
(Davey and Danly, Life's Meaning, and Something about Bats in a Cabin Wall)

If there only had been—

But there hadn't *only* been. And—

"No, Davey—careful! *Don't* put your fingers on a crack!" Lost Danly's voice chimed through his mind, plucked his hand from its descent. Between the broken chinking of the log cabin's wall, a bat could squeeze inside; along the roofline, wasps or flies or even spiders might get in; any creature to which the newer SARS—10, 11, the rumored 12—had spread could enter. Sealing every possible entryway, seeking ingredients from the dark pine forest to make into replacement sealant, spading for salvageable plants in what once had been a kitchen garden, keeping scavengers from raiding the fox traps (and how strange that the vulpine kind should thrive untouched though nearly every mammal on this Earth had already succumbed!), and struggling always to keep the sick alive another day—all of it chewed into their clearly too limited time. Trapping, sealing, struggling—and, in every "empty" moment, searching and digging for disinfectants—for, at least, whatever mirage of stock might be found (or not) in the dangerously distant ruins—each day was, to use Danly's old term, "a crapshoot."

"Only a lengthier dying," she had called it once, "like this hunger, this unending, necessary keeping watch and keeping-watch, and the terror and—oh Davey! our prickling anger at each other—us, you and me, love!—over such minor (until they turn lethal) slips . . . ." Oh yes, Danly's repetitious, intellectualized terms for . . . well, for everything, so that, lashing out (though only in words, never slapping, never striking at her, except that once), he'd shouted in reply, "This friggin' hell, you mean, this horror we're in—both of us, *both of us. Both* of us, Danly, so get with it! What you need is to *shut the fuck up.*"

Only the once, but that little moment—cracking something wide and deep, and surely more solid than the cabin's sturdy walls—had happened. Happened after only five weeks—out of 108 now? 818?—into this eternity where they had huddled, crowding together in this dark abandoned home, first shelter they had found from the second-wave SARS-n variations.

Sheltered indeed—for a time. Those first two years, between SARS-3 and, even, -8, when there'd seemed some possibility that, though the latest "iterations" had no cure, no vaccine possible, a partial "physiological mitigation" might be found, they had hoped that, even if they couldn't become actual doctors during such hardscrabble dearth years, someday there might again be arts, be hospitals, be a day to return to the work, to drive back to the lab, to observe . . . (*Oh, and how? And with what?*) There might again be people around, aiding one another, be life that led to something ("that can be for something," he'd cried out).

After the 11th variant, we still thought to salvage a remnant—were it only Danly's forceps or that half of little Mandy's photo we had saved from mildew during the Rain Year.

Davey laughed and laughed.

Those wonders, remember, your lives, were to doctor and heal. To trace new truths, to raise your and Danly's kids, to love little Ron, little Mandy, to—

He could barely stop laughing.

To love each other, to—

Instead, there'd been.

Pressed firmly into the crack, even this crude slurry could hold well, probably for several weeks. He had finished stirring it—the splintery, gravelly mix of wood and stone they'd used these years to patch the chinks and breaks. Used and used, despite the risks. Real risks—for logs must be retrieved and rocks be smashed, under the brooding, breeding rain. *Danly, Danly.*

Pushing with his left hand, he forced more slurry across the juncture's roughened surface and deep into the crack and the weakened patch beside it.

Instead, there'd been.

What there is. You could not save the kids, not help each other. Not save Danly. Not help anyone.

Meaning? Davey strained, listening. The static silence in the tight-sealed room, the emptied woods beyond the single, boarded window. Reaching down, he hauled the crate of slurry toward the hole that, in the crackling cold, today had opened under the window's sill.

Beatrice

It had been there, the fear, perhaps since she was born and certainly since she could remember. It was there in every recollection of those wallpapered rooms, those elegant overheated houses. It was there, later, in every season of what already seemed the middle years, years when she helped care for her father, wishing she had once told him of her admiration, but able only to sit embroidering another scarf and watch his mind decay—the last act, she had thought at the time, in that repetitious tragedy of futile brilliance.

Before then—long before—she had given up trying for another semester of university, ceased to hope she might write great works of philosophy, and instead gone to work to help pay her younger sister's therapy, her older brother's tuition. Later, many years after her father's death, when her mother, dependent and helpless as ever and now lacking a husband's shield, died, she had shouldered all the details of the funeral, the pain.

With her own children, she gave nights to feedings and illnesses, days to field trips and doctor appointments, waking moments to keeping the kids from knowing that "what's happening Over There"—in Europe, in the South Pacific—could still reach across the seas. She'd taken care of Reba through the girl's year of constant fevers and nightmares of "my schoolhouse burning" (surely pulled from newscasts about "bombed-out paper houses of Japan"), striving to protect the child from learning of the TB ("most likely encysted and won't become active illness"—but who could trust a Richmond doctor's diagnosis, and the War had moved Mel's entire bureau to this ignorant Southern city). At least they'd all loved the victory garden. And later—after the Bomb and after the War—those years when Reba was so terrified (it wasn't yet called "school phobia"), she'd let the girl stay home, striving to be less snappish with her but finding herself guilty of preferring Robbie, as quick and cuddly a child but more steadfast, her boy—though when the kids would bicker and argue, "Two is just right," she would remind them, "The elder gets praise, the younger gets kisses. But a middle child gets nothing."

She had thought, the War long over, the hard times behind them and the house mostly paid for, the kids both grown up, she and Mel might travel, and there would be time; but he died so soon. From the beginning, she was there, waiting through the long week in the hospital, protecting him as she had strived to protect her failing father, and (always ignoring that dread, as finally one must) soothing the children with long-distance calls — and never, then or since, in any way letting herself obligate them.

Afterward, though, it was time for herself. The dark old house was sold, the years of constant laundry and cleaning done. The new apartment, if rather small, shone and sparkled; her cotton curtains glimmered in the sunny kitchen; a cerulean pool gleamed in the building's courtyard down below. If it was now too late for scholarships, too laughable to "go back, at my age, to college," and, in any case, ambition pointless given that other knowledge—"too tiring," as she would quickly put it, glimpsing the familiar spectre hustling to emerge—still she might spend happy hours in simpler things, in visiting and shopping with friends, walking down these shaded streets with kindly, inquisitive new neighbors. At least between the back-to-back bouts, all winter long, of flu.

As soon as the weather cleared, she flew out to the Coast, visiting Rob and his wife and (that joy she had longed for, though perhaps not so much as to share her ideas) seeing her newborn granddaughter—not really her only grandchild, of course, but it was hard to fully count that unseen baby whom Reba had, all too grudgingly, twice mentioned "I gave up for adoption.

Rob's wife was reserved, however—more reserved

than ever—and so, to avoid imposing in their home, she finished by staying in a motel. When, in July, after yet another flu, she "split," as the kids would put it, to Europe to spend time with her unhappy daughter, Reba humiliated her in public, harshly and irritably, and in a hotel on Canne's rue du Verité in the middle of one night awakened her, "Mom, you snored." But she had determined to put up with her struggling daughter's moods, for Reba was secretly heartbroken, unable to speak up for herself with that too-charming Raoul, and thus again abandoned, and so "Goodnight, Reba dear," she had replied, and turned over in bed. Besides, she could not help the snores, just part of the sinus trouble that kept hanging on.

One evening, hours before she was to leave for the States, at a corner café near Metro Opèra they began finally speaking woman-to-woman, discussing, of all things, childbearing (how good that Reba come to confide in her!). Seeing their words were shocking the group of tourists at the very next table —American "Mrs. Grundy" types, she had thought but of course not said—they had broken into spontaneous momma-and-daughter laughter. Fifteen minutes later, as they parted, underneath the capital "M" of the Metro entrance, Reba turned and spontaneously grasped her in a bear hug.

But only that once, and how did they really feel about her, the children, their letters so perfunctory?

Or Mel's friends, who used to make baseballs of her "leaden" biscuits, those ages-ago summers at the beach? His family, with their constant criticisms? The people who would have laughed at what she might have tried to write—to say? And the nurses here, who, seeing that her brother knew the doctors, appeared so kind when they changed her i.v.? The intern, puffing out his shoulders, suggesting "perhaps a rabbi"? Didn't they understand she knew? No point, all that; the chicken's eyes must see its severed body flapping.

She would not bother anyone with her fear. Yet if nobody understood she had not meant to be a burden, that she had meant, rather . . . all those things she had not explained, this knowledge.

There was no way now to tell them. She would be dead soon; they might laugh on and on, and she could not change it.

It was this, she thought, struggling, what was meant by "the peace of the grave."

Wait!

Hah the meaning.

There were roses on the windows, in front of me now this wall, but roses here, if any, stiff on a volunteer's card. Here in November, "too young," (keep on thinking) "to die."

In front there is this wall. A sort of tan, with neither texture nor protuberance, nothing to hold the eyes nor is there any clock. Here there is no clock, but also no room-mate and I do not have to hear, except far down the corridors, the televisions. If the silence—but of course there isn't silence, people talking in the halls, carts in the night, lights.

Of course, but when there's no more light

"Eye oriented"—like looking at the bulkhead of the airline cabin, knowing any moment it might, in a final splintering.

Here, when I can open my eyes, is the tan wall. If there would be—as when, day or night, they turn me—only sky beyond that window. Only drapes, now often closed, the nightlight on the panes.

No, don't say that word. Dear God, dear God, please (I love you, amen), please let there be (not death, not dying, please You,) less or no more pain.

Dear God, I love you.

I do not want to die.

This is not news. Today I can think, this hour. Without hope. Without the foolish forced distraction. Without— when the pain worsens, I do ask for morphines; I will beg, have "earned" their disrespects. But now the doctor tells them Give, and the head nurse cares; there is hope

Hope for the dignity—minimum we

We who are dying or dead, no longer "they"—those who'll go on living.

I used to be among them.

When was it—age fifteen? I knew "Nothing matters," us animals, soon dead, our everything for meaning but "Hahhah it's 'basic' *in the language*." Later I would juggle, "Well, it's obvious, so what?" and, after years, see the meaning is the temporary, love, real *while we live*—and then the workdays and—our roses, roses by the front gate. We rented, never knowing, but the months years passed away, he walked, no longer toddling (I remember I remembered, as if long ago, when he was still a child)

But—bigger—the doctor has examined nurse took pulse and changed solution ("Wish there were a better vein"; they used to say "You have good veins," as if not simply a matter of time). Life is a matter of time.

It was to write immortalizing self (they'd say, or) "But she tried to do too much." *Who cares*? They can't immortalize. I'm about to be dead.

I already knew this—long before this, that, who wins who loses, soft stuff by fifty-plus known in our bones (Not to think about *bones*. Dear God, amen)

Listen— (Please. Amen)—the universe does not go on. But I wanted to live as long as. . . . "She didn't make it"; if I could believe this makes no difference and I didn't lose eternal

Well, you had your kids. Yeah so. I love you, Jesse, Carl. But you're not me; you know this. None of it saves. (And that's the point, or wasn't it?)

Sounds like a sick joke. I sound like a sick—

I am sick. Knowing "all this" doesn't save.

When I feel some comfort, joy takes mental flight and—

Yet it's not then comes the hope, or prayers (called bargaining). The hope in love or God, so I can believe there is, past death . . . Or if, if, *if* I only, and etc., then God, or nature or my body, karma, medicine, if I breathe right pray right think write right on or—again etcetera—will let me live

If only I'd not—! Sometimes I dream I'm back there, this hasn't happened

Then pain, or waiting for it

Help me.

It is when my body—when pain (not the worst yet) changes (or—no pattern really—) that the hope or "bargaining" builds.

Yeah. *Hope.* So I took the therapies. Pain weakness fear—dumb words. (Worms crawl, worms crawl) Took, tried, and it didn't work; I had hoped and I hoped, and now just morphine (please) (Dear God I love you. Amen.) And maybe

What is there, time going backward in outer space, each second itself like Earth rotating backward, thus such pain . . .? Will anybody (don't say *body*) care? "Hearing goes last"; will someone speak? And I hear, come back up to the surface. Will the worms and molds, bacteria, the body's—*my*—coagulation *hurt*? In what sense will brain's death be conscious, still be felt? No "I" left, is there still self's/non-self's agony? *How* will be that agony?

Will this movie (everything) stop first, or is there, under the last, last morphine, no end until more horror after/in the long (*how long*?) moment dying

Poetic, are we? (Trying to prepare?)

This is going to happen. To *me*, and to what is no longer "me."

Nurse—

Can't I lift this sheet? My arm hurts where the needle. The catheter— "She's asking help again. A screamer."
I don't want the agony. May pain not last, but be succeeded by beautiful (heavenly?) bliss before the end of everything.
(The circle of awareness slowly/quickly, like old movie fade-outs, shrinks.) What was important? Stopping a war, having my babies. Love, the children others.
Pink snow under Desolation.
Hands reach—
        (Only while we—)
"I"—but if even without (crawl in, crawl out) the eye (but isn't that beside the point?) And pushed past pain—
Enough allusion. Not illusion. "Point"? No.

No, what is this?
I don't want this.
Really. Please, a shot now, nurse.
    Please open the—
(roses where the wall wended)
                    Dear God

"Too late, she's—"

                    Here they come
this is ridiculous

                    Wait

Jenny's Garden

"Te gusta, esta jardine?" Jenny had reached the last page of the Lowrie novel ("no, not at all," she'd dare tell the argumentative nurse, "not actually trite or clichéd") and, looking up, had watched night's lowlit darkness fade to dawn, had listened to the moans and long cacophony of televisions as it spread around the ward, and heard the rising beep-beep-beep awaken the last sleepers, on that day.

Even now, she could remember—and how Jeffrey, then her "boyfriend" from the neighboring ward, also an Elder, had walked—walked!—through the doorway, fit and strong and saying "Up now, Jenny, wake, and rise!" and she had stood and glided toward him, glowing. Healthy. And amazed.

As all had been, in those first hours—first years, really. Yet the sole innovations required, as the headlines on the news sites in those days had proclaimed (along with lengthy, because nontechnical, explanations), had been three research teams' flashes of brilliance—the fitting together of a simple molecular splicing recognized since 2012 by geneticists at U.C. Davis and Institut Louis Pasteur (Paris 15ième), an earlier pre-trial procedure employing amazingly elementary electrolyte manipulations, and a (relatively complex) endocrine process employed since 1999. Et voila! No more cellular degeneration! Instantaneous whole-tissue regeneration! Perfectly calibrated immune response!

And then, mere days after that initial infusion of The Cure into the First World's entire population, Fast-Act took hold, enabling unimpeded reflexes and sensory perceptions matching those of the fastest human athletes—indeed, enabling speeds beyond that of the now-extinct cheetah, grips like those ascribed to "Big Foot" or gorillas, the flexibility of a Siamese cat, adaptability as swift as any insect's—in brief, "phase 2," as the Rockefeller Institute described it, of The Cure.

Jenny trembled in her joy and Jeffrey held her tight as she held him. "Oh yes," she sighed, and "Yes" he sighed as well, new-rising libido rushing through their loins, eyes tearing in forgotten tenderness.

So it began. And in those days, for those infused, there was no death. Nor for the chosen animals, nor trees, nor roses, nor of wheat or deep-rooted potatoes, nor of bees or fireflies or moths, nor cow nor horse nor stag upon the high-peaked mountains, nor of any other living thing. Except of what—fruit or egg or leaf or somehow broken stem or extra root—each life could share. And joy reigned.

Wandering through those years, eons latterly, Jenny walked—leaped, danced!—longhaired, lean, barefoot upon some eco-prairie of an Interstellar Liner's forward deck, en route to yet another planet of a long-discovered star amid some distant—ever more distant—galaxy. They sang, they made up tales, they weaved, they built a billion bridges, raised ten thousand homes, six hundred children on as many worlds. Life was an exploration, ever new and never fear-filled. Boredom, even "meaning," had no place—no place and no need—in this unending, well-loved, loving life.

For, unfearing, their love spread to many, to all life, in their universe. Their happiness. As here, lying together in the soft grass amid small yellow flowers, warm on this planet's high-country meadow between the whispering juniper and the sky-reaching grandfather pine.

A new dawn, Jenny thought, and "No, that's a cliché," and stroked, with two dusky fingers, Jeffrey's taut red-gold thigh. A child ran past them. Laughing softly, gently Jeffrey sighed.

No, harshly. Harshly. He had moaned.

Had cried out. Struggling, Jenny turned, lifted herself to one dark elbow, tried to lift her head, to find him in this pallid light, this painful dawn. The walls were still half-dark around her, figures still in shadow, groaning on their beds. As if in a tableau of "Age" and "Illness." As if bare archetypes of lone "Dying." As if each formed—again she thought—"a cliché." But, feeling as if falling, or rather as if the floor beneath her bed were turning, rocking forward and back as in an earthquake, she espied, below as well as above, the giant page she rode on lift, and turn—so that there, bright before her, lit as if by failing rays from some lost Eden, only, this time, clichéd, the words (oh utterly clichéd, and not at all like Lowrie's): "And then they awoke, and found it had all been a dream."

There Is a Silent Secret in the Woods of Ar-Cortiex

What I remember about Granma was she loved the silence, and she showed me, out on the high forest hillside, there beneath our own world's sun, what people used to call "birds."

Understand, this was on Ar-Cortiex III, back when I was just a kid and Daddy worked as a governor of the nine-planet Cortiex system. "See birdie," Granma'd tell me, and she'd point, say "birdie-birdie" and how big "in our thin air" those wings. And tell me, "Sylvie, know the forest sings a secret, but you got to go discover it yourself." I'd laugh and listen, and hear silence. Those were the days.

Back on Earth-Crowded'r, though, two decades later, after Daddy's death and my Marvin's, sick from Earth's thick air, we got forced to join the lined-up folk awaiting export ("exile," OakSing calls it—she's my tree-heart, brought from Cortiex, skinny-light like me and Granma, and all leaf-silk fur). It happened because-of Granma, mostly; she'd got so old and couldn't take Earth-loud noise.

Well, but like Momma's said, "That's Granma, too." Like me and Marv, you understand? Thin-air folks— grew up on Ar-Cortiex.

So, hearing now her crying here, crunched in that bed, tubes and stuff and scared, I hear those birds, hear the silence, forest back on Cortiex III. I remember how my little Granma took me out for treats, and now she's saying "Help me, help me—end me, Sylvie, no more this"; I know she means the noise—noise all around and always in these Hospi-Crowds on Earth. I say, "Granma, yes I'll try." I can't, though, cannot stop it—not Earth noise.

It started with that tooth, you understand? Infected— before then, back on Cortiex where our "air's so thin/ ya wanna spin," Granma was strong and happy. But here, especially with their "20 + 11 days'" wait per appointment, that tooth got really, really bad; those microbes simply "climbed her bones/got up so high/ they sought the sky," as OakSing told me, and doctors stuck her right away into a Hospi-Crowd. So Granma—oh they kept her life up, kept her ears on, all that, but—she's never been the same. And so now every day she's here, my Granma, locked into the Hospi-Crowd, where all the televisions and "dumb-games all play/ all night and day"—and every other moment, too, bzzz-thump-bzzz-zhppp, no stop to it.

And they drugged her up, of course, since she shout-ed, "Stop your loud noises! Let me sleep!" which is not allowed. To shout—that's not allowed, not in crowds. It bothers folks, here on their Earth.

Me? I've sent Josie and my Momma out to exile over Delta Ariadne, sent Kalie and the boy along with. They'll be okay; there's grass and cows and woods on Delta, peo-ple say. "The sky is blue, the trees are pink/ the snakes don't climb out of the stink"—you understand? They'll be okay.

But I stay here with Granma. I take her on my lap, then sigh and carry her out through the corridors' bang-bang, past televisions, televisions, televisions blaring and the guys' construction noises all 'round each bend. I car-ry her on—on beyond.

And then I put her on my lap again, here out on Last Meadow (more like a square), and I put OakSing right beside her too, so now she lies back to hear Cortiex's mu-sic of the heart; and, in 'spite of every throbbing from their noisy tractors, and in 'spite she's got her palm across her mouth to hide all those lost teeth, she smiles. And I say, "There. You comfortable, Granma? No need we ever be going back." And she smiles some more. And taps my finger, the one that used to carry Marvin's ring, and says . . . too low. So I ask, "What's that, Granma?" and she draws, with her skinny fingers, six words.

Bless you. You found it. Love.

Time Speaks

Urrrr . . .

Lonely as I was, who'd turned her quest to primal natural law or mathematics and the ordinary language ("One wouldn't say 'consolations'") of philosophy, and later trudged the roadside dust in struggle for some universal—and her own—deep love and peace, I finally was forced, dismissing every book and every well-meant character or cat who (I believed, or doubtless) loved me, as well as each persona, lost or cultivated, and endeavor, and all hope, to place the trusting creatures and creations in some country of the heart; then, unencumbered by words' artifice or ancient compass, by "possessions" or "possessors," Torah or Bhagavad Gita, I embarked.

Even now, we use that metaphor, *embarked*, and speak of spaceships. Yet that elegant machine—crowded, old-fashioned, Oxfordian in its dark patinas of deep oak and walnut wood—that *bateau vif* on which I raced, fleeing as much my love for one person as his lack (real or imagined, rational or feared) of love for me—yet fleeing, even more, my knowledge that each love must end and has no certainty, and that life, too, must end and be as if unbegun—fleeing, that is, from tragedy and comedy and every other challenge that, across the elegance of time, had turned to paradox whatever I had known: *bref*, that "machine" of my unutterable flight, that great and "singular" mathematical computer and traverser of coordinates upon the outer/(inner) sky on which I, with the (bravely trembling-hearted) others (!) of our expedition rode, was no more a ship than . . .but here I want to say: than was the painted ship of Coleridge's ocean. Although Einstein has been, as laypersons put it, "proven wrong"—though it is possible, and we were able, to traverse great distances of space and arrive at precharted suns "traveling faster than the speed of light" (or, as the purists put it, "'traveling'. . .")—though, with no verifiable changes in our mass, our units of measurement, or our synchronization with what is/(was?) called "Earth time", and above all with no disruption or inundation of the eternal processes of the Silent galaxy, we were able to arrive at the 300,000 light-years distant e3-Aurigae system in about 333 Earth-days; and yet that machine in which we traveled, along however Euclidean trails, was not (though/while hardly a "time machine") a *ship*. As Earth is not an island, nor the comprehension of that green and gentle globe "sufficient unto itself," neither did we traverse any oceans "westward" nor to continents or poles.

Yet if "behind" me were the long despairs of love, the desolate days of what were known as ordinary pains and sorrows, and every loss and terror of the shrunken late and later years of life, which either to comprehend or to miscomprehend must prove perhaps false or empty, I had left behind, as well, the beloved(s) whose voice(s) had challenged my certainties and asked me the impossible (however a seeming salvation may have lain hidden in these words): to ask nothing, nor to judge what leads us all to final loss. This meant to not try to comprehend myself, or humanity, or life on Earth.

I fled our common globe that I need not flee my mind.

*

It is not entirely false to say that, on the 333rd day of our "trip", we "arrived at" the third ("third") planet of e_3-Aurigae, and found it to be inhabited. Even though the proposition would be, by all that is native to our nature or our language, doubted, yet I must add that, with these "soft-eyed, sad-voiced," understanding, warmly "human" natives, we were able to establish communication.

I and Janzie—my sweet, kindhearted Janzie—beamed in our reflection of their bright-toothed smiles.

*

"To understand a person's language," remarked the twentieth-century philosopher Ludwig Wittgenstein, "is to understand their way of life." To elucidate this supposition, the philosopher constructed many models, "savage tribes" whose "language games" (and, we might say, whose *understanding*) contained at best the rudiments of ours. And a fiction writer of that century, one Jorge Borges, created (as a speculative construction) a world-within-worlds the inhabitants of which began their "knowledge", their "understanding", of events (which by them would not be termed "events" at all) from the logic and terminology of what we would consider Philosophical Idealism. To think of an object *sincerely* was, that is, to create it, and of course to create it upon, within, the "reality" of that (Borges's) world; "object", "actual object" were, in short, despite the linguistic system based upon Idealism, words of significant meaning to those (albeit fictional) inhabitants.

But in these years, as well, the mathematician Gödel had already published his (to date undisputed) proof of the impossibility of proving, within any logical system sufficiently complex to contain a statement of its own completeness, that completeness itself; to do so, according to this derivation (itself a meta-proof in a system isomorphic, or logically identical, to our common-usage mathematical field), was necessarily to create at least one contradiction, and thereby a totality of contradictions, within the system. In short, proof of completeness (of a system's capacity to prove or disprove "all things" stateable—that is, thinkable—within it) must imply the destruction, within this system, of all consistency and proof.

Again, during that century the English author George Orwell had related an imaginary 1984 where, through control of press, video, and other communications, and indeed of the very language and syntax of thought, a ruling elite, themselves de facto animated robots of an autonomously governing System, controlled not only all understanding of past, present, and therefore future history—of the very existence of so-called verifiable events (and thus, naturally, of the participants)—but the citizenry's actual perception or belief in even such "primary" elements of knowledge (language, rationality, reason) as, for example, "2 + 2 = 4". Under sufficient pain and fear, to survive beneath a virulent tyranny's inescapable judgment, any person would deny, eventually, not only feeling and its objects but also prerequisite integritous thought.

It is true that also, in those early years, the Canadian Atwood would touch more optimistically on this position—on, that is, the role of love in overcoming "rational" blocks—and the work of Olsen came to hinge upon the very *un*certainty of causative influence, while the author Le Guin would form, upon her detailed worlds, tribes and societies of inexpressible empathic bases (welcoming always in the deep-imagined languages of their own/"Other" life forms); and indeed thinkers everywhere were describing not only denial but also acceptance in the face of catastrophic or even "ordinary" death, millennia after centuries of mystics treated both of common and of holy love.

However, it is not as affectation or with mere nostalgia that I mention "now" these classic, beloved works (although they "numbered" among the volumes that I'd left, undertaking this journey, behind). No, I relate, unhappily briefly, such indubitably abstract or fictional sketches, or models, of worlds so that it may be—or (I must unhappily admit) might have been—possible to make palatable, somehow comprehensible, the results of our discoveries on Rrrr. . .

*

The first thing I would try to tell you is that the inhabitants of the peculiar, beautiful world of Rrr . . . (those "huge-eyed, all-accepting," and "somehow," we thought, "contradictory, egoless—open, childlike, yet deeply mature, tragedy-laden, ephemerally wise"—forever laughing *beings*) both spoke and thought in a language whose logic was *totally different* from ours. In no way could their axioms, their mathematics, the very syntax of their language and systems of knowledge within *any* language (once these, by the necessary-to-translation processes of "being-with," of "joining-in-with," the inhabitants' way of life began to be understood)—*in no way* could their comprehension (I am tempted to say: their rationalities) be made noncontradictory, be found even partially equivalent, to the logic and reasonings of Earth. Moreover, *it was the logic and language of these* (oft-lost, youthful-yet-aged) *inhabitants of Rrrrr that in actuality applied* to the facts, the events, the entities and objects, each heartbreaking circumstance, of their planet. (It is necessary, as may be imagined, that I speak—or, was it

Janzie who spoke [so dear and gone beloved]?—in considered metaphors.)

On Rrr. . ., for example, 1 + 1 = 3, 2 + 2 = 6, 2 x 2 = 5, 3 / 5 = 10, (although 1 x 1 is, as with us, 1) (at least at "first"), and while the Rr. . . ian processes of "addition", "multiplication", "counting" are no more a *creating* or physical *cause* of the obtained answers than are the equivalent processes in our Earthian mathematics, yet— let me repeat this—the results, strange as it may seem, are by no means a mere game or amusing formal structure but, rather, apply exactly to each event, each measurement, each quantity of objects on that world.

As if we from Earth were fragile, precious children, the inhabitants of Rrrrrr, kindly creatures ("with," we said, "the tragic eyes of those who know they are doomed, the helpless resigned silence of all to whom our nature's law, *Be fruitful and multiply*, comes with too great difficulty— or too great an ease")—these gentle beings took us, as if miraculous, newborn souls, into the very classrooms of their world and taught us all they knew—of counting, of addition, of such elementary logical propositions as "An object is what it is not," "An object is not what it is, or is it"; these simple tautologies/truisms were presented, in accordance with standard Rrr. . .ian methodology/ies, by the equally ordinary pedagogic processes of "counting," "describing," "playing with," "grouping," "coming to understand," "adding up," "caring for/ merging for/being with," our peers and contemporaries—who included, in our case, not only certain particularly warm or wise or witty (may I dare say loved?) among the Rrr...ians but (obviously) our dear comrades, every member of our expedition.

(O Janzie! David, Ari! How/where/whether—?)

You see, it was in this simple, basic procedure—as well as, to be sure, our protracted attempts to map the size and mass and coordinates, the towering/shortening heights of those flashing peaks and numbers of the labyrinthine river, or rivers, of Rrrr. . ., as well as in our longing (sudden, somehow breaking us) to reach to and fully *know*, to achieve some deeper, closer (even intimate!), *lasting* terms with individual ("individual") Rr...ians—indeed to find or hold or merge in trustful unity with, "be-with"— even "be"—these soft-furred, nonjudging, encompassingly loving "ones"—that, becoming finally, suddenly aware of the danger and the glory of our exploration, we—I—all of me's/you's—did, at length/in no time, realize our ("your," "her"/"his") "own" life's/(lives'}/gift's/(gifts') disaster(s).

*

Where, or whats, my (y/our) ship(s) ("ship") may be, or what, within some system of (non-)Euclidean coordinate(s), it might mean for "us" again to "traverse distances" (I speak in metaphorz) on sweeping "voyages" across outer (inner?) 'space', I cannot say. These must say everything of Rrrr; that am, say nothing(s). But if, like seafaring rescuers of shipwrecked wanderers of "old"— or if somewhere my books lie open on (some) shining floor/s, my cat/s in certainty of supper purring, lovers, ghosts or friends, and neighbors gathered round—if thus, from some lost purpose/ings, you would come save us, then I tell you: Rrrrrrr. . ., not difficult to find (where and whatever it may be), is also known, at least to their inhabitant(s), by two three many other names; some call it Death some call it Life, in full uncertainty and warmth, and one is "Chaos," "Night," and one (should thought be long, or hope be lorn) begins sometimes with G sometimes with J sometimes with none, and changes "always" its "length" of "letters(ss)s)s)," know/have meaning/s numerous or innumerable, listentome/us/you, still your

or/of meninglsnesness, meens must be awway outt in r time isthuscomplex lovor thn ovyer or ofwrds yr—isno-morenow?

Inthisreachbeyondyearscares loveto/for oneanother, elsetherofbe silent. Mennglsns losscrygv lifelov

vy vy vayv' Ha Who

*

It may be this sporadic manuscript thus ends, as do we all (though others claim the rest *is/was* [*conceived*] or in lost specie/s' script). A few have argued that these "pages'" final words ("these" "'pages'" "'final'" "word/s'") denote

Whoever you are who found this, reach beyondlove forto

. .

The consolation of your memory

www.ingramcontent.com/pod-product-compliance
Lightning Source LLC
Chambersburg PA
CBHW021323190726
48288CB00003B/941